T. Frederick (Thomas Frederick) Ball

Queen Victoria

Scenes and Incidents of her Life and Reign

T. Frederick (Thomas Frederick) Ball

Queen Victoria
Scenes and Incidents of her Life and Reign

ISBN/EAN: 9783337059040

Printed in Europe, USA, Canada, Australia, Japan

Cover: Foto ©Raphael Reischuk / pixelio.de

More available books at **www.hansebooks.com**

QUEEN VICTORIA:

Scenes and Incidents of Her Life and Reign.

BY

T. FREDERICK BALL.

With Ninety-four Illustrations.

TENTH EDITION
(Seventieth Thousand).

TORONTO, CANADA:
TORONTO WILLARD TRACT DEPOSITORY:
A. G. WATSON, MANAGER.

1888.

PREFACE

O.V the 20th of June, 1887, Queen Victoria will, we trust, complete the fiftieth or Jubilee Year of her reign, and in anticipation of that time, it has been thought that a book descriptive of the chief scenes and incidents of her life might suitably be published. Owing to the seclusion in which the Queen has mostly lived for some years past, many of the present generation have never seen her, and have no very vivid idea of her as a real person. Whether or not they will know her any better after reading this volume remains to be seen. It is not intended as a book for children, but for those young people who are old enough to take an intelligent view of facts and events. At the same time it is hoped that it will meet with acceptance at the hands of those who can remember many of the events here briefly recorded.

It should be borne in mind that this is not exactly a life of Queen Victoria. I have chosen out interesting facts and circumstances from a great many different sources, in order to give my readers some personal idea of the illustrious lady who rules over our island home. If it is looked upon in the light of a biography of the Queen, it will be found that I have left out a great deal more than I have put in. It may serve, however, to awaken an interest which my readers can gratify with the perusal of more voluminous works as they get the opportunity.

And here I must gratefully own my indebtedness to Her Majesty's own deeply interesting *Leaves* and *More Leaves*, to Sarah Tytler's *Life of the Queen*, to the *Diary of Royal Movements*, and many books, magazines, newspapers, etc., from which I have culled the facts I needed for the preparation of this volume.

CROWN JEWELS.

CONTENTS

CHAPTER.   PAGE.

  I. THE OLD PALACE AT KENSINGTON 13

 II. INFANCY AND CHILDHOOD 23

III. ON THE STEPS OF THE THRONE 35

 IV. THE MAIDEN QUEEN 47

  V. THE CORONATION 65

 VI. COURTSHIP AND WEDDING 77

VII. HOME LIFE 85

VIII. ATTEMPTS ON THE QUEEN'S LIFE 95

 IX. ROYAL BABIES 105

  X. VISITS TO SCOTLAND AND FRANCE 113

 XI. STATE CEREMONIES AND FESTIVITIES 121

XII. ROYAL LIFE IN THE HIGHLANDS 129

XIII. THE QUEEN IN IRELAND 143

XIV. "ALL NATIONS" IN HYDE PARK 151

 XV. IN THE ISLE OF WIGHT 165

CHAPTER.   PAGE.

XVI.   THE WAR CLOUD 173

XVII.   DOMESTIC EVENTS 185

XVIII.   SORROW UPON SORROW 193

XIX.   THE COMING OF ALEXANDRA 203

XX.   ILLNESS OF THE PRINCE OF WALES, ETC. 217

XXI.   ANECDOTES 235

HER MAJESTY'S MOTHER, THE DUCHESS OF KENT.

From a Print by]

[*Messrs. P. D. Colnaghi & Co., Pall Mall.*

From a Photo]　　　　　　　　　　　　[by Messrs. Downey.

QUEEN VICTORIA.

CHAPTER I.

THE OLD PALACE AT KENSINGTON.

GEORGE III.

THE old red brick palace at Kensington does not strike one as a very beautiful object when viewed from the outside. The great Sir Christopher Wren had something to do with planning it, but then he had to consider the Dutch tastes of his employer, and although the brickwork—simply considered as brickwork— is said to be remarkably good, the general effect is not picturesque. But for all that the old Palace is still a very comfortable dwelling place for royal folks, and about its courts and halls and galleries a great many associations thickly cluster. It has always had the credit of being a homely, domestic sort of place rather than an abode of regal

splendour. That lively writer, Leigh Hunt, says :
"Windsor Castle is a place to receive monarchs
in; Buckingham Palace to see fashion in; and
Kensington Palace seems a place to drink tea in."

There is an old tradition which says that in the
time of Henry VIII. there was a royal nursery
upon this site. If such was the case, Queen
Elizabeth and Queen Victoria may both have
passed their earliest years on the same spot.
However that may be, we know that William III.
took a fancy to a house that was standing here in
his reign, and bought it of the owner, Lord
Nottingham. The King considerably enlarged the
mansion and altered it to suit his own tastes, until
he had created for himself a regular Dutch palace
in a Dutch garden. Here the blunt, taciturn
monarch, sorely vexed because after all his trouble
he might not use England at his pleasure as a mere
pawn on the European chessboard, often held his
dull Court. till his wife Mary and himself were
successively carried from this Palace to their
graves. Then came Queen Anne, sitting in quiet
stupidity with her fan in her mouth, waiting so
anxiously for dinner to be announced, and scarcely
speaking three words at a time to anybody; whilst
through her Court moved Bolingbroke, Swift,
Addison, Steele, Prior, and others, whose very
names give lustre to the story of her reign. Nor
must we forget that extraordinary Sarah Jennings
(afterwards Duchess of Marlborough) who knew
so well how to manage her royal mistress.

George I. improved the Palace, and George II. made it his chief residence. The last-mentioned King was very fond of having his own way in everything; and when his ministers saw that it was not for the good of England that he should have it, these old walls often saw strange scenes. The monarch used to work himself up into a dreadful passion and tear his wig to pieces, whilst Queen Caroline quietly waited for her royal spouse to get reasonable.

This irritable King died suddenly as he was sitting at breakfast in Kensington Palace one morning in 1760. His successors on the English throne, having more commodious and more attractive homes elsewhere, have as a rule left Kensington to their relations. Here lived the good and patient Princess Sophia, the blind daughter of George III. Here for a few years resided the unfortunate and misguided Caroline, Princess of Wales, and under the rule of that pleasure-loving woman and her companions Kensington Palace knew, perhaps, the gayest period of its history.

Passing over various illustrious occupants, we find in 1819 a portion of the old Palace occupied by the Duke and Duchess of Kent. The Duke of Kent was the fourth son of George III., and was superior to any of his brothers in all that commands admiration or respect. His cordial sympathy with the spirit of progress that was increasingly manifesting itself in the country, his mental ability, his upright character, and his amiable and generous disposition won for him the esteem of all right-minded Englishmen. Unfortunately, the oligarchy that then ruled England feared and hated the liberal sentiments of this enlightened Prince, and they meanly punished him for his progressive ideas by keeping him financially in a straitened condition, although ready enough to vote immense sums of public money for the maintenance of the extravagance and profligacy of his brother, the Prince of Wales. The Duke of Kent had married in 1818, Victoria Mary Louisa, a Saxe-Coburg Princess, widow of the Prince of Leiningen. She was also a sister of Prince Leopold, beloved of the English people, and of whom I shall have a word or two to say presently. The Kents had but one child, a girl, born at Kensington Palace on May 24th, 1819. That little girl grew up to be Queen Victoria of England.

And now let us pause for a moment and look back at that year 1819, when the illustrious lady was born, who now sits upon

" Her throne, unshaken still,
Broad based upon her people's will
And compassed by the inviolate sea."

When first her baby eyes opened to the light of day in the old Palace at Kensington, the nations of Europe were at peace—a long, long era of fire and sword had come to a close in the three days' carnage of Waterloo. The great disturber of the nations, Napoleon, was pining on the rock of St. Helena, with ample leisure to meditate upon the

seas of blood with which he had deluged the soil
of Europe. There was great distress in England;
the wicked Bread Tax was in force, and many
cruel things were done to keep down the people
when they met together to try and get old-
fashioned wrongs set right. The poor old King
George III., blind and crazy, was gradually
nearing the tomb to which Queen Charlotte (his
wife for more than fifty years) had been borne in
the previous year. The Prince Regent was re-
velling at Carlton House. In the world of science,
Sir Humphry Davy took the highest place; whilst
the prominent names in literature were: Scott,
Byron, Shelley, Keats, Wordsworth, Coleridge,
Southey, Campbell, Moore. The slave-trade had
been abolished, but Catholic Emancipation, the
Repeal of the Corn Laws, the Reform Bill and
other great works had yet to be accomplished.
Lord Ashley (afterwards Earl of Shaftesbury) was
at this time a youth of eighteen, and, of course,
not yet in Parliament, so that his long career of
philanthropic triumphs, which we have so lately
seen brought to a close, was still in the future, and
the many wrongs which he attacked and conquered,
were flourishing unchecked. As it is intended to
make the present sketch of Queen Victoria's career
as far as possible a personal one, future allusions to
political or general topics will be few and brief,
but a rapid glance round before beginning the
story seemed desirable.

And next it will be well to say a word or two

about the baby's ancestors. On both sides the
royal infant could claim a grand pedigree. Her
father was the son of the reigning monarch, and
could trace back his descent through a long line
of Kings and Princes, to Alfred the Great. Her
mother's family, the Coburgs, showed an un-
broken descent for nine hundred years from a
Saxon Earl, Theodoric. A notable man amongst
these Coburg ancestors was Frederic the Wise,
Elector of Saxony, one of the first German Princes
to accept the doctrine of the Reformation, and a
powerful protector of Martin Luther. About a
hundred years previously there had been another
Elector, Frederic of Saxony, who had his two
children kidnapped by a rebel knight. But the
children were recovered, and the rescue was chiefly
due to the exertions of a brave charcoal-burner
who, with the pole used in his business, fiercely
belaboured the rebel knight. For this day's
services, the right of cutting from the royal forests
such wood as they needed in their business
operations was granted to the charcoal-burner and
his heirs for ever, as well as a nice farm and an
annual allowance of corn. All these privileges
are still (or were till very lately) enjoyed by
the descendants of the charcoal-burner. "Our
Gracious Queen" is twelfth in descent in a direct
line from Ernest, the elder of the two kidnapped
and rescued children.

When Princess Victoria first saw the light in
Kensington Palace, it was by no means a certainty

that if she lived to be a woman she would be Queen of England. The Regent's daughter, Princess Charlotte of Wales, had not long before been laid in the grave after eighteen months of happy wedded life at Claremont. Her husband, Leopold of Coburg, afterwards King of the Belgians, went home stricken with sorrow, whilst England was mourning for the hope of the nation cut off in her youthful prime. Still more recently, the Princess Victoria's Uncle and Aunt Clarence had lost their first little infant princess. Still, the Clarences might have other children, and if so, they would be nearer to the throne than the child of the Duke of Kent. But Kent always looked upon his daughter's high destiny as a settled thing, and he delighted to hold up his little girl and say, " Look at her well, she will yet be Queen of England!"

When a month old the little Princess was baptised with great pomp in the grand saloon of Kensington Palace. In order to do all proper honour to her small Royal Highness, the royal gold font was brought from the Tower, and the Archbishop of Canterbury and the Bishop or London came to perform the ceremony. There had been some little fuss about finding a name for the baby—the father wanted to call his child Elizabeth, thinking it was a name that would please the people, if she came to occupy the throne. But the Prince Regent said that he and the Emperor of Russia would be godfathers, and the child should be named Georgiana Alexandrina,

B

after the pair of them.   Happily this doom was
escaped, and the little Princess was duly christened
Alexandrina Victoria.   Uncle Leopold, heartsore
from his recent bereavement, and shrinking from
all public ceremonials, nevertheless constrained
himself to be present.

From Winterhalter's Coronation Painting.

[*To face Chap. II*

CHAPTER II.

INFANCY AND CHILDHOOD.

GEORGE IV.

EITHER at Kensington or Claremont the Princess Victoria chiefly spent the first years of her life, but visits to watering-places and other attractive spots were by no means unfrequent. Indeed, she began her travels at a very early date, for she was barely six months old when she was taken to a pretty spot near Sidmouth, on the Devonshire coast, to spend her first winter. Here, at the beginning of 1820, the Princess had her first narrow escape from being killed. A boy who was shooting at sparrows near the house managed to send a charge of small shot through the nursery windows, and some of the shot actually passed close to the head of Princess Victoria, who was in her nurse's arms.

But of her danger and of her narrow escape the child was of course unconscious, and equally so of the real calamity that befel her a few days afterward. Her father, the Duke of Kent, came in one day with his feet wet after walking in the grounds, and instead of changing his things at once he lingered playing with his baby until a chill struck him. Severe inflammation of the lungs set in, and in January, 1820, he died. And now there began for the Duchess of Kent that long widowhood of forty-one years, during which the great purpose of her life seemed to be to watch over the career of the daughter left in her charge. The story of Queen Victoria and her eventful reign could never be rightly told without a tribute of praise to the noble-minded woman who moulded the character and trained the hopes and aspirations of England's future Queen. Uncle Leopold came at once in the hour of sorrow, took back the widow and her child to their home at Kensington, and, with true brotherly kindness and generous help, softened the difficulties of the position.

We get a peep at Princess Victoria and her mother a few months after the sad event just alluded to, in a letter written by William Wilberforce (the friend of Africa) to Hannah More. He says, " In consequence of a very civil message from the Duchess of Kent, I waited on her this morning. She received me with her fine animated child on the floor by her side with its playthings, of which I soon became one. She was very civil, but as she did not sit down I did not think it right to stay above a quarter of an hour; and there being but a female attendant and a footman present, I could not well get up any topic so as to carry on a continued discourse. She apologised for not speaking English well enough to talk it; but intimated a hope that she might speak it better and longer with me at some future time."

The old King George III. had died six days after the Duke of Kent, and soon afterwards the Duke of York's wife died, leaving no children, so the throne was gradually coming nearer and nearer to the little Princess at Kensington. But in December, 1820, the Clarences had another baby, who was styled Princess Elizabeth Georgina Adelando, and who, if she had lived, would in all probability have become Elizabeth II. of England. But in a few months the weakly infant passed away, and Princess Victoria—or "little Drina," as she was then called in the family—was again, though knowing nothing of her high destiny, in a fair way for being Queen of England.

The little Princess was only about three years old when she again had a narrow escape from being killed. She was thrown out of a pony-carriage which her mother was driving in Kensington Gardens; and the carriage was just

falling over on the child, when a soldier caught at
her dress and swung her into safety. The soldier
was rewarded for saving the "little Drina," and
the Duchess of Kent took down his name and
regiment and promised to do something more for
him. Five pounds were sent to the man afterwards
when on duty in Ireland, but it was not till
November, 1877, that John Maloney found out that
the Princess Alexandrina, whose life he had saved
fifty-six years before, was the same lady that had
come to be Queen of England.

The routine of life in the old Palace at Kensington is thus described by a writer in *The Queen.*
"The life of the Duchess and her children at
Kensington was plain and simple. The family
party met at breakfast at eight o'clock in summer-
time, Princess Victoria having her bread and milk
and fruit put on a little table by her mother's side.
After breakfast Princess Feodore and Princess
Victoria went out for an hour's walk or drive.
From ten to twelve her mother instructed her, after
which she would amuse herself running through
the suite of rooms which extended round two sides
of the Palace, and in which were many of her toys.
Her nurse was a Mrs. Brock, whom the Princess
used to call her 'dear, dear Boppy.' At two
came a plain dinner, while the Duchess took her
luncheon. After this, lessons again till four ; then
would come a visit or drive, and after that the
Princess would ride or walk in the gardens, or
occasionally, on very fine evenings, the whole

party would sit out on the lawn under the trees. At the time of her mother's dinner the Princess had her supper laid at her side; then, after playing with her nurse, she would join the party at dessert, and at nine she would retire to her bed, which was placed by the side of her mother's."

The Princess Feodore mentioned in the above extract was the beloved half-sister of our Queen, being the Duchess of Kent's child by a former marriage. Before passing on, we must take another peep at the royal infant, as described in the columns of a newspaper of the period. The writer tells how he saw in Kensington Gardens "a party consisting of several ladies, a young child, and two men-servants, having in charge a donkey, gaily caparisoned with blue ribbons, and accoutred for the use of the infant." He soon found that the Duchess of Kent and her daughter formed the centre of the group. "On approaching the royal party, the infant Princess, observing my respectful recognition, nodded and wished me a good morning with much liveliness, as she skipped along between her mother and her sister, Princess Feodore, holding a hand of each." She was careful to return all salutations as she passed along. "Her Royal Highness," continues the writer, "is remarkably beautiful, and her gay and animated countenance bespeaks perfect health and good temper. Her complexion is excessively fair, her eyes large and expressive, and her cheeks blooming. She bears a very striking resemblance

to her late royal father, and indeed, to every
member of our reigning family."

In the summer months (like a great many other
children in less exalted families) Princess Victoria
was often taken to stay at the sea-side. We have
seen her at Sidmouth, and next year she was at
Brighton, lodging in that extraordinary edifice, the
Pavilion ; and afterwards she was several times at
Ramsgate, which became a very favourite spot,
both with her mother and herself. A writer in
Fraser's Magazine tells us how he saw the Princess,
when five years old, playing on the Ramsgate
sands in her simple dress—"a plain straw bonnet
with a white ribbon round the crown, a coloured
muslin frock, looking gay and cheerful, and as
pretty a pair of shoes on as pretty a pair of feet as
I ever remember to have seen." Near by stood
her mother, conversing with William Wilberforce,
and laughing when an unexpected wave suddenly
rippled over the feet of the Princess. The writer
we are referring to watched the Duchess and her
daughter proceed up the High Street to their
residence, and saw the child run back to put some
silver in the lap of an old Irishwoman sitting on a
doorstep.

Passing on a couple of years, we get a glimpse
of the appearance of Princess Victoria when seven
years old, from Lord Albemarle's *Autobiography*.
He says, "One of my occupations of a morning,
while waiting for the Duke, was to watch from
the windows the movements of a bright pretty

little girl, seven years of age. She was in the
habit of watering the plants immediately under
the window. It was amusing to see how im-
partially she divided the contents of the watering
pot between the flowers and her own little feet."
She was usually dressed in "a large straw hat and
a suit of white cotton; a coloured fichu round the
neck was the only ornament she wore."

Early in 1827 the Duke of York died, and the
Duke of Clarence was now heir presumptive.
During the last illness of the Duke of York, his
little niece, Princess Victoria, visited him daily,
always carrying in her hand a bouquet of choice
flowers. In the summer of that year, the well-
known author, Charles Knight, passing along the
broad central walk of Kensington Gardens, "saw
a group on the lawn before the palace, which to
my mind was a vision of exquisite loveliness. The
Duchess of Kent and her daughter, whose years
then numbered nine, are breakfasting in the open
air—a single page attending upon them at a
respectful distance—the matron looking on with
eyes of love, whilst the 'fair soft English face' is
bright with smiles." About a year afterwards,
another writer, Leigh Hunt, gives us a picturesque
glimpse at England's future Queen. He writes:
"We remember well the peculiar kind of personal
pleasure which it gave to see the future Queen, the
first time we ever did see her, coming up a cross-path
from the Bayswater Gate, with a girl of about her
own age by her side, whose hand she was holding as

if she loved her. A magnificent footman in scarlet came behind her, with the splendidest pair of calves in white stockings which we ever beheld. He looked somehow like a gigantic fairy, person- ating somehow for his little lady's sake the grandest kind of footman he could think of; and his calves he seemed to have made out of a couple of the biggest chaise lamps in the possession of the godmother of Cinderella."

Of the early life of Princess Victoria, simplicity and regularity were very marked features. There was plenty of out-door exercise as well as plenty of good teaching and diligent study. Her Royal Highness rather objected to regular instruction at first, and (something after the style of her grand- father, George III.), was inclined to ask, "What good this?" "What good that?" but was soon convinced of the need for learning and accom- plishments. Like many other children, she was very fond of pictures and objects of interest, and was especially gratified by a visit to the British Museum, not then despoiled of its natural history collections. Through the wise training of her excellent mother, her mental powers were solidly developed, and not merely devoted to the acquire- ment of showy accomplishments. Her frequent journeys, and as she grew older, her visits to the country mansions of the nobility, all tended to increase the child's powers of observation. She was always expected to finish whatever she was doing before she began anything else. This rule applied even to her amusements. Once, when playing at hay-making, she flung down her little rake and was running off to seek some other amusement, but she was made to come back and finish the hay-cock she had begun before she was allowed to go away.

The Duchess of Kent made it a special point to inculcate exact truthfulness, and her daughter proved an apt pupil in learning this important lesson. One morning she had been very impatient and indeed refractory during her lessons. The Duchess coming in asked the governess, Baroness Lehzen, how the Princess had behaved. The governess said, "Oh, once she was rather troublesome." Princess Victoria gently touched her arm, and said, "No, Lehzen, *twice*, don't you remember?"

Considering her position, the Duchess of Kent was left in but poor circumstances, and, indeed, but for Prince Leopold's liberal help, would have been much straitened. The household arrangements were of necessity conducted with a business exactitude, and a regard for economy in striking contrast to the spendthrift extravagance which was so conspicuous in other branches of the royal family. The Princess had her allowance and was expected to make it suffice and never to overrun it. Once at the Bazaar at Tunbridge Wells, in the year 1827, she had expended all her pocket money in a number of presents for various relations and friends, when she remembered another cousin, and saw a box marked half-a-crown which would be just the

thing for him. The bazaar people wished to
enclose it with the other articles purchased. But
the governess said : "No! you see the Princess
has not the money, and so of course she cannot buy
the box." The offer was then made to lay it aside
till purchased, and the Princess thankfully assented.
As soon as quarter-day came round she came to the
bazaar on her donkey, before seven in the morning
and carried the box away with her.

In 1828 sister Feodore was married to an upright
and excellent man, the Prince of Hohenlohe. There
was a grand wedding, and then the inevitable
parting.

Princess Victoria had not often visited her uncle,
George IV. We hear of her paying a visit to
Windsor in 1829, and respecting this visit her
Coburg grandmamma wrote: "The little monkey (!)
must have pleased and amused him, she is such a
pretty clever child." Princess Victoria was again
at Court when a splendid children's ball was given
in honour of the child-queen of Portugal, Donna
Maria II. la Gloria. This grand little woman with
the grand name fell down and bruised her face
when she came to dance, and had to be taken away.
But our Princess did not often find herself amongst
these gaieties, for her prudent mother very wisely
kept her away as much as possible from the dis-
reputable Court of the worst of the Georges.

ARRETON CHURCH, ISLE OF WIGHT.

CHAPTER III.

ON THE STEPS OF THE THRONE.

IN the year 1830, William IV. ascended the throne of England. Notwithstanding his high position as the ruler of a mighty nation, this monarch often displayed the manners of a rough sailor, and when he was excited or vexed, he frequently used to swear dreadfully. This sort of thing did not at all suit the refined ideas of the Duchess of Kent, and so she still kept her little girl as much as possible from the Court. The Duchess, however, kept up a sincere friendship with the King's wife, good Queen Adelaide. The

WILLIAM IV.

summer of 1830 was spent by Princess Victoria and her mother amongst the pleasant hills of Malvern. We believe the townsfolk have been telling visitors ever since how the Queen, when a girl, used to ride about Malvern on a donkey, and enjoy herself just like any other healthy, happy English girl. During the same summer, Princess Victoria was also taken to Birmingham, Kenilworth Castle, and some other places of note in the Midlands.

The first State appearance of Princess Victoria at Court took place in February, 1831, on the occasion of a grand drawing-room held by Queen Adelaide. In the midst of all that brilliant throng, the chief centre of attraction was the girl of twelve in her frock of English blonde, standing in simple dignity beside her aunt, the Queen, and taking an interest in all that was going forward. "We can without difficulty," says Miss Tytler, "call up before us the girlish figure in its pure white dress, the soft, open face, the fair hair, the candid blue eyes, the frank lips, slightly apart, showing the white, pearly teeth."

The English Parliament, seeing that Princess Victoria was now next heir to the Crown, gave her mother ten thousand pounds a year, which made things rather more comfortable. Her twelfth birthday passed before the Princess was made aware of her high position. She had been very carefully guarded, and sharp questions as to why the gentlemen bowed to her and not to her sister

Feodore, and so forth, had had to be evaded somehow. But the time had now come when it was
deemed right fully to reveal her prospects to her.
A genealogical table was accordingly placed in
the historical work used by the Princess. Her
governess, Baroness Lehzen, tells us how " Princess Victoria opened the book as usual, and, seeing
the additional paper, said, 'I never saw that
before.'

" 'It was not thought necessary you should,' I
answered.

" 'I see I am nearer the throne than I thought.'
" 'So it is, madam,' I said.

" After some moments the Princess answered,
'Now, many a child would boast, but they don't
know the difficulty. There is much splendour, but
there is much responsibility.'

" The Princess having lifted up the forefinger of
her right hand while she spoke, gave me that
little hand, saying, 'I will be good. I understand
now why you urged me so much to learn even
Latin. My aunts, Augusta and Mary, never did ;
but you told me Latin is the foundation of English
grammar and of all the elegant expressions, and
I learned it as you wished it ; but I understand
all better now.' And the Princess gave me her
hand, repeating, 'I will be good.' I then said,
'But your aunt Adelaide is still young, and may
have children, and of course they would ascend
the throne after their father, William IV., and not
you, Princess.' The Princess answered, 'And if

it was so, I should never feel disappointed, for I
know by the love aunt Adelaide bears me how
fond she is of children.'"

The coronation of William IV. and Adelaide
took place in the following September, and everybody was surprised that Princess Victoria was
absent. The *Times* and other papers made a great
deal of fuss about it, but the matter was soon
explained. The Princess had recently had more
publicity and excitement than was good for her
health, and so her mother on this grand occasion
kept her quietly at home.

During the next year or two, whilst England was
so full of wild excitement about the Reform Bill,
and the great Duke of Wellington who had been
almost worshipped as a successful warrior was
getting hated as a statesman, Princess Victoria
was quietly getting on with her studies. That
these studies were some of them difficult, we have
already seen. No pains were spared to fit her for
the high duties which it now seemed so certain she
would be called upon to fulfil. She was evidently
a bright quick-witted little maiden. One day she
was reading the well known anecdote of the
Roman matron, Cornelia, pointing to her sleeping
children as "My jewels!" "She should have said
'My cornelians,'" was the passing remark of the
Princess. Like most other children, Her Royal
Highness was sometimes a little wilful. She did
not always feel in the mood for pianoforte practice,
and she was one day told that there was no royal

road to perfection and that only by very much practice could she become "mistress of the piano." The Princess at once closed the piano, locked it, and put the key in her pocket. "Now you see there is a royal way of becoming mistress of the piano" she exclaimed. But having had her little joke, she was soon persuaded to resume her practice.

In the summer of 1831 the Duchess of Kent and her daughter spent three pleasant months at Norris Castle in the Isle of Wight, and the Princess began to love the fair island so intimately connected with the joys of later years. Miss Greenwood tells us of a tourist who happened to visit Arreton Churchyard at the time we are speaking of, and who on nearing the tomb of the "Dairyman's Daughter" found a lady and a young girl sitting beside the mound. The girl was "reading aloud in a full melodious voice the touching tale of the Christian maiden." He found afterwards, on speaking to the Sexton, that the two ladies were the Duchess of Kent and Princess Victoria.

But the Princess had at times to figure in scenes of a more exciting character than the quiet church-yard of Arreton. She was only about twelve when she opened the Victoria Park at Bath—her first experience of a duty to be undertaken times without number in after life. Now and again she stayed at the Pavilion at Brighton, and walked on the Esplanade, where she had the opportunity of learning not to mind being stared at. At Wentworth House and Alton Towers and Chatsworth and other mansions of the nobility, she was an honoured guest, and in her progresses to these places she was taken to inspect cathedrals and colleges and factories, and had to listen whilst prosy addresses were read by mayors, etc., to her mother at various towns they passed through.

There is a curious little anecdote told of Princess Victoria on the occasion of her visit to Wentworth House, the seat of Earl Fitzwilliam. One morning, after a rainy night, she was running about the grounds, when an old gardener who saw her on the point of descending a sloping piece of lawn, called out "Be careful, Miss, it's slape!" " What's slape?" said the Princess; but almost immediately her feet slipped from under her, and the future Queen measured her length on the damp grass. The old gardener hastened to help her up, and in reply to her question, gravely said " That's slape, Miss!" So royal people, like other folks, often have to learn by experience.

On the thirteenth birthday of Princess Victoria, a grand juvenile ball was given in her honour by the King and Queen. There was a large number of the children of the nobility present, and Queen Victoria in later years spoke of the scene as one that made a deep impression upon her. All the Kensington tradespeople illuminated their houses in honour of the young Princess, whom they knew so well. A few days afterwards she was at a Drawing Room; but she was not often at Court,

and King William IV. began to get jealous of the
secluded way in which she was brought up, and
also of the popular demonstrations that greeted
her when she went about the country.

During 1833, the Princess and her mother spent
some months in the Isle of Wight, at Norris Castle,
and in the yacht "Emerald" visited several towns on
the South Coast. During one excursion the Princess
again had a narrow escape from being killed. A
gale had come on suddenly, and she was watching
the stirring scene when the topmast was heard
to crack. The pilot sprang to the Princess and
lifted her to a place of safety, and immediately
afterwards the mast came crashing down on the
very spot where she had been standing. That
pilot got promoted; and at his death, some years
later, his widow and family were provided for by
Queen Victoria.

There were no photographs at that time in the
shop windows, although certainly there were
pictures of royal people more or less like them.
Still, comparatively few people knew Princess
Victoria by sight, although everybody had heard
of her; so she could easily go about unnoticed.
One day she was in a jeweller's shop, when she
saw another young lady looking at some gold
chains. This young lady had selected one she
was evidently anxious to purchase, but presently
she laid it down reluctantly and bought a cheaper
one. When the young lady had gone, Princess
Victoria made some enquiries, and then ordered

both the chains to be sent to the young lady's address. In the packet the Princess placed her card with a few words written on it expressing her pleasure at seeing prudence and self-denial, and requesting her to accept as a present the chain originally selected.

About this time the American writer, N. P. Willis, saw Princess Victoria standing beside her aunt, Queen Adelaide, at Ascot Races. "The Queen," he says, "is undoubtedly the plainest woman in her dominions, but the Princess is much better looking than any picture of her in the shops, and for the heir to such a crown as that of England, quite unnecessarily pretty and interesting."

The Princess and her mother visited the Northern parts of England in the summer of 1835. On their way home they were at a grand ball at "Burghley House, by Stamford Town," the seat of the Marquis of Exeter. At the dinner there was a great bustle because an attendant managed to upset a pail of ice into the Duchess of Kent's lap. Three hundred people were at the ball afterwards; it was opened by Princess Victoria and the Marquis of Exeter, and then, after her *one* dance, the Princess, like a good girl, went off to bed.

In the following year, Princess Victoria saw, for the first time, her future husband, Prince Albert of Saxe-Gotha, and his brother Ernest. They were cousins to the Princess, with whom they spent a very pleasant month at Kensington. They were taken to see all the sights of London, and were

present at grand drawing-rooms and balls, and so
forth. Sometimes these young Germans, who
were used to simple, early habits at home, were
kept up so late at State dinners, etc., that, as Prince
Albert afterwards confessed, it was sometimes with
the utmost difficulty that he could keep awake.
But he had to get used to all that sort of thing in
after years. Leopold (who had now become King
of Belgium, and who was uncle to both the young
people,) had set his heart on making a match
between Victoria and Albert, but nothing was
settled just at present, and the two young men
went back to their studies at Bonn University.
But amongst the Queen's rings, Lady Bloomfield
says there is one, a small enamel with a tiny
diamond in the centre, given to her by Prince
Albert when he first came to England, a lad of
seventeen.

In the autumn of this year, the Duchess of Kent
and the Princess stayed some time at Ramsgate.
This was the last seaside holiday they had together, before the daughter was called upon to
accept the cares and obligations of royalty. On
May 24th, 1836, the Princess reached her
eighteenth birthday, and accordingly came of
age, for royal folk in England are allowed that
privilege three years earlier than other people.
There were serenades and balls, and illuminations,
and all sorts of holiday doings. Kensington
seemed almost beside itself with flags everywhere,
and bells ringing and bands of music playing.

But the old King was too ill to be at the grand ball at St. James's Palace in the evening, and the faithful Queen would not leave the sick-room. The ball was a very brilliant affair; Princess Victoria danced in the first quadrille with young Lord Fitzalan, afterwards Duke of Norfolk, and father of the present Duke. She also danced with the noted Austrian Prince, Esterhazy, whose Court dress sparkled with diamonds from head to foot. It was said that whenever he wore this splendid dress, a great many gems were dropped without his knowing or caring. The Princess had many fine birthday gifts; amongst others a magnificent grand pianoforte, worth two hundred guineas, from the King. Next day there were addresses presented congratulating the Princess; and amongst the rest one from Birmingham, brought up by a good man, named Thomas Attwood, who, in a very solemn and earnest manner, spoke a few words, which caused the Duchess of Kent to be deeply moved. At this time Baron Stockmar arrived at Kensington. He was a wise, just, and benevolent man, who had been King Leopold's secretary, and was now sent to act as confidential adviser to Princess Victoria.

King William did not recover from the illness just now spoken of. At the earliest dawn of day on June 20th, 1837, he breathed his last. With all his coarseness and obstinacy, we have had many worse kings.

CHAPTER IV.

THE MAIDEN QUEEN.

WE have said in the last chapter that the old King died at earliest dawn. The birds were in full song in Kensington Gardens when the Archbishop of Canterbury and the Lord Chamberlain and four other gentlemen came from Windsor with the news.

VICTORIA.

Miss Wynn, in her *Diary*, says: " They knocked, they rang, they thumped for a considerable time before they could rouse the porter at the gate. They were again kept waiting in the courtyard, then turned into one of the lower rooms, where they seemed forgotten by everybody. They rang the bell and desired that the attendant of the Princess Victoria might be sent to inform Her Royal Highness that they requested an audience on business of importance. After another delay and another ringing to enquire the cause, the attendant was summoned, who stated that the Princess was in such a sweet sleep that she could not venture to disturb her. Then they said, 'We are come on business of State to the Queen, and even her sleep must give way to that.' It did, and to prove that she did not keep them waiting, in a few minutes she came into the room in a loose white nightgown and shawl, her nightcap thrown off and her hair falling upon her shoulders, her feet in slippers, tears in her eyes, but perfectly collected and dignified."

After the announcement had been made, the first words spoken by the young Queen were to the Archbishop of Canterbury: " I beg your Grace to pray for me ! " They knelt down together, and so with prayer to God the new reign was inaugurated.

The next thing was to write to the widowed Queen Adelaide at Windsor. The letter was full of sympathizing condolence and affection, and the writer earnestly begged her dear Aunt to stay at Windsor as long as she pleased. It was noticed that the letter was addressed to " Her Majesty the Queen." Someone who had a right to speak observed that this was not correct and that it should be directed to Her Majesty the Queen-Dowager.

" I am aware of that," said the girl-queen ; " but I will not be the first to remind her of her altered position."

The Queen got away at length to finish her toilet and talk over matters with her beloved mother. But at nine Lord Melbourne, the Prime Minister, came, and then a Privy Council was summoned for eleven. Princes and peers and high officers of Church and State came to that Council, wondering how the royal girl, of whose inner nature so little was known, would demean herself. England had seen women mount the throne—Mary was thirty-seven, Elizabeth twenty-five, and Anne thirty-eight at their respective accessions—but the present case was something altogether different.

The Council met—a large assembly of the foremost men in England. How the young Queen read the speech Melbourne had prepared for her, and how she passed through the long ordeal of a multitude of men swearing allegiance and kissing her hand, I need not describe in detail. Sir David Wilkie and other artists have painted the scene of that " First Council of Victoria." When her aged uncles, the Dukes of Cumberland and Sussex, knelt to do homage, she was visibly affected, but through all the rest of the ceremony she charmed all beholders with her calm simplicity and dignity. There was a Mr. Greville present who has written a spiteful diary full of all the bad things he could say about everybody, but even he could only praise on this occasion. He says, " Never was anything like the first impression she produced or the chorus of praise and admiration which is raised about her manner and behaviour, and certainly not without justice. It was something very extraordinary, and something far beyond what was looked for."

Respecting Wilkie's picture of that First Council, we find him thus writing to Collins: "In October I received a message from the Lord Chamberlain to attend the Queen at Brighton, with a view of beginning the Embassy picture, but was told the Queen had heard of a sketch I had made of her First Council. Accordingly, on seeing Her Majesty, and finding her strongly set upon this, I sent for a canvas from London, and began the figure of the Queen at once. She is placed nearly in profile at the end of a long table covered with red cloth. She sits in a large chair, or throne, a little elevated, to make her the presiding person. Having been accustomed to see the Queen as a child, my reception had a little of the air of an early acquaintance. She is eminently beautiful, her features nicely formed, her skin smooth, her hair worn close to her face in a most simple way; glossy and clean-looking. Her manner, though trained to act the Sovereign, is yet simple and natural. She has all the decision, thought and self-possession of a queen of older years; has all the buoyancy of youth, and from the smile to the unrestrained laugh, is a perfect child." Among other well-known figures, the picture contains the portraits of the "Iron Duke" and the Duke of

Sussex, Lord Melbourne, Lord Lansdowne, Lord John Russell, and Sir Robert Peel.

The young Queen had to receive visits from many noble personages before this busy exciting day was over. Meanwhile, in the City the great bell of St. Paul's was tolling, and flags everywhere were half-mast high, and shops were partially closed in memory of the King who had passed away.

On the following day the ceremony of the Proclamation took place. The Queen, suitably escorted, passed through the streets crowded with her subjects to St. James's Palace, where according to custom she had to make her appearance at a certain window. Around her were great lords in their State robes, and many of the nobility were visible at other windows. The Quadrangle below was tightly packed with favoured spectators. The Queen was dressed in deep mourning, with a white tippet, white cuffs, and a border of white lace under a small black bonnet, which was placed far back on her head exhibiting her light hair in front simply parted over her forehead. Her mother stood beside her and watched her tenderly, as now and then the young Queen seemed moved by the acclamations of her subjects.

Garter King-at-Arms, with heralds and pursuivants in their robes of office, were posted in the court below. Here, too, were officers-at-arms on horseback, bearing massive silver maces; sergeants-at-arms and sergeant trumpeters with their maces and collars, and other officers. Presently Garter

King-at-Arms read the Proclamation, announcing the accession of Queen Alexandrina Victoria to the throne of these realms—"to whom we acknowledge all faith and constant obedience, with all humble and hearty affection, beseeching God, by whom kings and queens do reign, to bless the royal Princess Alexandrina Victoria with long and happy years to reign. God Save the Queen!"

Then the band struck up the National Anthem, guns were fired in the Park close by, and answered by the guns at the Tower, and the acclamations in the Palace Court were taken up by the thousands outside, till it seemed as if a great thrill of joy spread over London and thence over all the land at the accession of the Maiden Queen.

At that supreme moment of triumphant hope the girl's feelings were too much for her, and she fell upon her mother's neck and wept. Concerning this incident the gifted poetess, Elizabeth Barrett Browning, thus writes:—

> "O maiden, heir of kings,
>   A king has left his place;
> The majesty of death has swept
>   All other from his face;
> And thou upon thy mother's breast
>   No longer lean adown,
> But take the glory for the rest,
> And rule the land that loves thee best.
>   The maiden wept,
>   She wept to wear a crown.

    •   •   •   •

God bless thee, weeping Queen,
   With blessings more divine,
And fill with better love than earth
   That tender heart of thine ;
That when the thrones of earth shall be
   As low as graves brought down,
A piercéd hand may give to thee
The crown which angels shout to see.
   Thou wilt not weep
   To wear that heavenly crown."

About three weeks after the proclamation, Queen Victoria bade farewell to her Kensington home, and went to reside at Buckingham Palace. Never did royal Princess changing her residence leave behind her a more pleasant memory. In a cottage at Kensington lived an old soldier servant of the Duke of Kent. The Duchess and her daughter used often to visit the family, in which there were two children in ill health. The little boy died, the girl lived an invalid. Soon after the Queen left Kensington, a clergyman happening to call, found the girl in a very cheerful mood. The new Queen had sent a copy of the Psalms, marked in the margin with the dates on which she herself used to read them, and containing a pretty marker worked by the royal hands. This is only a sample of the kind and considerate conduct which made the people regret their lost Princess, even while they shared the universal joy at her accession to the throne.

Her Majesty's predecessors had been Kings of Hanover as well as of England, but as the Salic

Law, which forbids a woman to reign, was part of the law of Hanover, the Queen's uncle, the Duke of Cumberland, became King of that country. It

was no real loss to this country, and no doubt we escaped a good deal of trouble by getting rid of all territory on the continent of Europe.

On July 17th, the Queen went to prorogue Parliament. She was drawn for the first time by

the famous cream-coloured horses from the royal
stables, and went to sit upon the throne of her
ancestors in the House of Lords. Then she read
her speech proroguing Parliament. The noted
actress, Fanny Kemble, was present, and gives us
a clear impression of what the Queen was like at
that time. She says : " The Queen was not handsome, but very pretty, and the singularity of her
great position lent a sentimental and poetical
charm to her youthful face and figure. The serene,
serious sweetness of her candid brow and clear
soft eyes gave dignity to the girlish countenance,
while the want of height only added to the effect
of extreme youth of the round but slender person,
and gracefully moulded hands and arms. The
Queen's voice was exquisite, nor have I ever heard
any spoken words more musical in their gentle dis-
tinctness than 'My Lords and Gentlemen,' which
broke the breathless silence of the illustrious
assembly, whose gaze was riveted on that fair flower
of royalty. The enunciation was as perfect as the
intonation was melodious, and I think it is impossible to hear a more excellent utterance than that
of the Queen's English by the English Queen."
The sturdy republican, Charles Sumner (who came
prejudiced against the Queen), is equally warm in
his praises, and there is abundant independent
testimony to show that the young Queen was a very
lovely girl, charming all sorts of people by her
affability and grace.

I need not refer to the numerous deputations

from various bodies that thought it necessary to assure the young Queen of their loyalty and good wishes; but one of these was, perhaps, of a more interesting character than the majority. I allude to the fifty members of the Society of Friends appointed to present Her Majesty with an address which contained, in addition to the usual professions of loyalty, an expression of their hope that she would be guided by the principle of peace. As is well known, the Friends object to uncovering the head, as a mark of respect or inferiority, before persons of distinction, even before royalty itself. The accompanying engraving shows the manner in which this difficulty was surmounted. As the Friends passed up the broad staircase of St. James's Palace to Queen Anne's Chamber, they had to pass, two by two, between a couple of Yeomen of the Guard, who gently lifted the hat of each Quaker as he passed and put it aside until the ceremony was over. The well-known Friend, Jacob Post,. has written a description of the presentation and the incidents connected therewith, which appeared in *The Welcome* for 1879.

At the elections both Whigs and Tories used the name of " Our young Queen " as a war cry, but we need not linger over all this. One of her first cares, now that abundant means were hers, was to pay all her father's debts and the advances which English noblemen had made to her parents to enable them to keep up a royal position in the land. She knew that her mother's embarrassments

WINDSOR FROM THE RIVER.

[To face Chap. IV.

THE QUAKER DEPUTATION TO THE QUEEN.

D

had been due to her own requirements as heir to the throne, but, personally, she had never been sixpence in debt in her life.

In the earliest period of her reign, the Queen rose at eight, and was very soon occupied in signing despatches and other routine business, which occupied her till breakfast-time, at a quarter to ten. An attendant was then sent to invite the Duchess of Kent to breakfast with the Queen. Without this special summons the Duchess never approached her daughter, and she was careful never to speak about State affairs. All this etiquette was needful to avoid giving cause for suspicion of undue influence. At twelve noon the Queen met her ministers, and the Council was succeeded by riding or walking exercise. There was a select company at dinner, and in the drawing-room afterwards the Queen took her part in singing or playing, in both which accomplishments she was proficient.

One Saturday night, in this first year of Queen Victoria's reign, a certain noble minister came at a late hour to Windsor. He informed the Queen that he had brought down some documents of great importance for her inspection, but that, as they would require to be examined in detail, he would not encroach on Her Majesty's time that night, but would request her attention the next morning. "To-morrow is Sunday, my lord," said the Queen. "True, your Majesty, but business of the State will not admit of delay." The Queen then consented to attend to the papers after Church the next morning. The nobleman was somewhat surprised that the subject of the sermon next day turned out to be the duties and obligations of the Christian Sabbath. " How did your lordship like the sermon ?" asked the Queen on their return from Church. " Very much indeed, your Majesty," was the reply. " Well, then," said the Queen, " I will not conceal from you that last night I sent the clergyman the text from which he preached. I hope we shall all be improved by the sermon." Sunday passed over without another word being said about the State papers, until at night, when the party was breaking up, the Queen said to the nobleman, " To-morrow morning, my lord, at any hour you please ; as early as seven, my lord, if you like, we will look into the papers." His lordship said he would not think of intruding upon Her Majesty so early as that, and he thought nine o'clock would be quite early enough. " No, no, my lord," said the Queen, " as the papers are of importance I should like them to be attended to very early ; however, if you wish it to be nine, be it so." Accordingly, at nine o'clock next morning, the Queen was in readiness to confer with the nobleman about his papers.

Another anecdote referring to the same period may be related here. It was at that time the Monarch's duty personally to sign death warrants. A court-martial death warrant (says Miss Green-wood) was presented by the Duke of Wellington

to the Queen to be signed. "She shrank from the
dreadful task, and with tears in her eyes, asked—
'Have you nothing to say on behalf of this man?'

"'Nothing; he has deserted three times!' replied
the Iron Duke.

"'O, your Grace, think again!'

"'Well, your Majesty, he certainly is a bad
soldier, but there was somebody who spoke as to
his good character. He may be a good fellow in
private life.'

"'O, thank you!' exclaimed the Queen, as she
dashed off the word 'Pardoned' on the awful
parchment, and wrote beneath it her beautiful
signature."

Acts of a similar character on the young Queen's
part led Parliament to arrange for the fatal signing to be performed by Royal Commission. The
avowed reason was "to relieve Her Majesty of a
painful duty," but, in fact, her tender woman's
heart was not to be trusted in such an awful piece
of business.

Old folks, who were in their teens in the first
year of Victoria's reign, can well remember the
loving loyalty that seemed to thrill all classes of
the community, even those who were agitating
about grievances. The great O'Connell declared,
in thunder tones, "If necessary, I can get 500,000
brave Irishmen to defend the life, the honour, and
the person of the beloved young lady by whom
England's throne is now filled." Charles Dickens
(who had just written the *Pickwick Papers*) was

for a time almost beside himself about the young Queen. Some men really went crazy, and took to haunting the outside of the palaces and the Queen's drives quite unpleasantly.

In the autumn of 1837, the Queen took possession of " Royal Windsor;" and upon those stately terraces, and as mistress of those lordly halls and towers, rich in historic associations, and grand with the trophies of ancient and modern chivalry, she must have felt that she was Queen of England indeed.

On November the 9th, the Queen attended the Lord Mayor's Banquet at Guildhall. This was her first visit to the City of London, and it was a memorable occasion. In a dress of splendid pink satin, shot with silver, and with a diamond tiara on her head, the Queen rode through dense crowds of her loving subjects, who greeted her with enthusiastic cheers. At Temple Bar the Lord Mayor gave Her Majesty the keys of the City, and she graciously returned them, and then the Lord Mayor and Aldermen, etc., joined the procession and escorted their Queen through the City streets. At St. Paul's, the scholars sang the National Anthem, and the senior scholar delivered an address. Of the splendid banquet and the grand company, there is no need to say much. Her Majesty was pleased to make the Lord Mayor a baronet, and to knight the two Sheriffs. One of the latter was Sir Moses Montefiore, the first Jew who ever received the honour of knighthood from a British

Sovereign.   Our readers will remember that he
died only the other day at the venerable age of

nearly 101, full of years
and honour.   A fortnight
afterwards the Queen
went, in State, to open
her first Parliament.   The
sum of £385,000 a year
was voted as the income
of the lady who a few
years before had had to
leave the purchase of a

SIR MOSES MONTEFIORE.   half-crown box till next

Quarter-day.   But it must be remembered that a
very large portion of this great sum of money
was for salaries and expenses not under her immediate control.

It is a curious fact that, out of the large income
above mentioned, the sum of one shilling and
fourpence should, on one occasion, not have been
forthcoming when required.   The Royal Family
had to pay toll, like other people, for crossing
Battersea Bridge, and one day the Queen and
fifteen persons rode across; the last in the *cor-
tége* was a groom, from whom sixteen pennies
were demanded.   He happened to have no money
with him, and he accordingly handed a silk handkerchief to the turnpike man as a pledge, which
he afterwards had to come and redeem.

H.R.H. VICTORIA, PRINCESS ROYAL OF ENGLAND, AND CROWN PRINCESS OF GERMANY.

[To face Chap. V.

THE REGALIA.

CHAPTER V.

The Coronation.

D URING the first part of the year 1838, great prepara-tions were made for the ap-proaching Coronation. It was agreed to alter in some respects the ancient ceremonies, and to dispense with the six hundred kisses on the left cheek from "the Lords Spiritual and Tem-poral" which would have been according to precedent. The old Crown used by George IV. and William IV. weighed seven pounds, and was too large for the Queen's head. So another was made of less than half the weight— a cap of blue velvet with hoops of silver, brilliant with diamonds, pearls, rubies, sapphires and emeralds. Above it rose a ball covered with small diamonds, surmounted by a Maltese Cross of brilliants, with a splendid sapphire in its centre. In front of the Crown was another Maltese Cross bearing the enormous heart-shaped ruby, once worn by Edward the Black Prince. But we cannot further particularise the ornaments of this splendid diadem, and will only add that the precious stones of all sizes numbered 2,166 and were worth nearly £113,000. The famous Koh-i-noor had not yet been obtained.

For many weeks, or rather months, beforehand, little else but the Coronation seemed to be on people's lips. There were coronation songs and hymns, coronation medals, coronation ribands, and so forth. At length the eventful day arrived, and on the 28th of June the dawn of day was announced by the firing of guns in St. James's Park and at the Tower. As early as five in the morning a few carriages were proceeding towards the venerable Abbey of Westminster, and between six and seven the western streets of the Metropolis were thronged with strings of vehicles and streams of eager pedestrians. The streets were gay with decorated balconies and seats in every available position. At the edge of the pavement were long lines of horse or foot soldiers, and military bands were stationed here and there. At ten o'clock a salute of twenty-one guns proclaimed that the Queen had just left Buckingham Palace. She was in her

grand State carriage, drawn by eight cream-
coloured horses, and tremendous were the loyal
acclamations of the people as she passed along.
Very enthusiastic, too, was the cheering that
greeted the Duchess of Kent, for it was universally
felt how great was the debt of gratitude the nation
owed to the illustrious lady who had so well
prepared her daughter for her high career. The
royal carriages formed part of a long procession,
for ambassadors, and royal princes and other distinguished personages and high officials were all
there in carriages; and then, too, there were
trumpeters and watermen, and yeomen and hunts-
men, and marshals and foresters, etc., as well as
squadrons of Life Guards and their bands. As the
procession passed on through the streets—where
side-walks, balconies, windows, and the very roofs
(where possible) seemed alive with spectators
waving scarves and handkerchiefs, and shouting
their loyal greetings—the sight was one never to
be forgotten by those who witnessed it.

We must briefly glance at the scene within the
Abbey, for to describe it in detail would fill too
many pages of our little book. The old stone
pavement of the long Nave was hidden from sight
with purple and crimson cloth, and on each side
stood a line of tall Life Guards, just above whose
waving plumes were the temporary galleries
covered with crimson cloth and gold fringe, and
accommodating about a thousand persons. In the
Choir, on a platform covered with cloth of gold,

stood the superbly gilt Chair of Homage facing the altar. Nearer to the altar, which was gleaming with massive gold plate, stood the Chair of St. Edward, in which so many English monarchs have sat. Beneath it was the celebrated "stone of destiny," used in past ages for the coronation of Scottish kings, and declared by some to be the very stone on which Jacob laid his head at Bethel. Round about were galleries tapestried with green and gold, and accommodating the ambassadors, members of the House of Commons, judges, and other distinguished persons. The peers and peeresses occupied the transept.

If we bear in mind that a large proportion of the gentlemen present were either in military or official attire, that the ambassadors, especially, were gorgeously arrayed, Prince Esterhazy (for one) being covered with diamonds, even on the heels of his boots; that the peers were in robes of State, and the peeresses in beautiful dresses, and flashing back the sunshine from thousands of precious gems, we shall realise a little the brilliancy of the spectacle. And to vary the scene there were the members of the Choir in surplices and white dresses, and quaintly attired "gold-sticks" flitting about, and trumpeters perched up aloft, and above all the venerable Abbey roof and the glorious windows bright with the morning sun. Harriet Martineau, who was present, says: "About nine, the first gleams of the sun slanted into the Abbey and presently travelled down to the peeresses. I had never before seen the full effect of diamonds. As the light travelled each peeress shone like a rainbow. The brightness, vastness, and dreamy magnificence of the scene produced a strange effect of exhaustion and sleepiness."

Some of the peeresses had been five hours in their seats when at twelve o'clock to the sound of triumphant music the grand procession swept along the Nave. There were princes and ambassadors and great nobles bearing the regalia; but the chief interest of course centred in the young Queen, now "a royal maiden of nineteen, with a fair pleasant face, a slight figure, rather small in stature, but showing a queenly carriage, especially in the pose of the throat and head." She walked up the Nave escorted by two Bishops, and wearing a royal robe of crimson velvet furred with ermine and bordered with gold lace, and having a gold circlet on her head. Eight beautiful daughters of English dukes bore her train, and fifty ladies of rank holding offices in the Queen's household followed.

As the procession passed into the Choir a few moments delay occurred. The Turkish Ambassador was struck with bewilderment at the splendid spectacle and had to be courteously woke up and moved on to his seat.

Every one rose as the Queen advanced to the centre of the Choir, the musicians sang the anthem, "I was glad," and the Westminster boys from their gallery chanted "Vivat Victoria Regina." There was silence for a few moments as the Queen knelt

in private devotion, and then began the first ceremony, the "Recognition." The Archbishop of Canterbury presented Victoria as "undoubted Queen
of this realm," and was answered by shouts of "God
save Queen Victoria." Divine service followed,
in which several prelates took part, and then there
was a sermon by the Bishop of London. The
Queen next took the oath to maintain the law and
established religion. The "Anointing" followed.
Four Knights of the Garter (dukes and marquesses)
held a canopy of cloth of gold above the Queen,
whilst the Archbishop anointed her head and hands
with oil. After the orb and ring and sceptre, etc.,
had been given to the Queen with the customary
ceremonies, the Archbishop offered prayer, and then
reverently placed the crown of these realms upon
the Queen's head. Then from all that great concourse rose the shout of "God save the Queen," and
the Peers and Peeresses put on their coronets. The
effect of the flashing jewels as this act was performed was startling in its brilliancy. At the same
moment trumpets pealed forth and drums were beat,
and the loud boom of the cannon at St. James's Park
and the Tower resounded through the City.

The Queen was then enthroned in the Chair of
Homage. The Archbishop, on behalf of himself
and the other spiritual peers, first knelt and did
homage. The Princes of the blood—the Dukes of
Sussex and Cambridge—touched the crown of their
royal niece, took the oath, kissed her on the left
cheek and retired. Then came the long train of

peers—seventeen dukes, twenty-two marquesses, ninety-four earls, twenty viscounts and ninety-two barons—each in turn touched their Sovereign's crown and knelt and kissed her hand. To one peer, Lord Rolle, the task was a very difficult one. "The large infirm old man," says Miss Martineau, "was held up by two peers, and had nearly reached the royal footstool when he slipped through the hands of his supporters, and rolled over and over down the steps, lying at the bottom coiled up in his robes. He was instantly lifted up, and he tried again and again, amidst shouts of admiration at his valour. The Queen at length spoke to Lord Melbourne, who stood at her shoulder, and he bowed approval ; on which she rose, leaned forward, and held out her hand to the old man, dispensing with his touching the crown. He was not hurt, and his self-quizzing on his misadventure was as brave as his behaviour at the time." Lord Rolle was over eighty years of age. Some facetious person informed a foreigner who was present, and the latter gravely reported it to his own countrymen that the Lords *Rolle* held their title on condition of performing this feat at every Coronation.

After partaking of the Sacrament, and undergoing a few closing ceremonies, the Queen left the Abbey at a quarter to four. She had "spent nearly five hours in being finished as a Queen," as Miss Greenwood puts it. And now, with the crown on her head and the sceptre in her hand, she rode back to her Palace, and her shouting subjects saw that Victoria was really now their crowned Queen.

"Poor little Queen!" said Thomas Carlyle, with rugged kindliness, "she is at an age at which a girl can hardly be trusted to choose a bonnet for herself, yet a task is laid upon her from which an archangel might shrink."

The artist, Leslie, sat, as a Royal Academician, not far from the throne, and took notes for a picture of the scene. He tells us how the Queen, who was very fond of dogs, had a favourite little spaniel who always looked out for her return when she was from home. On the day of the Coronation she had, of course, been separated from the little dog much longer than usual. "When the State coach drove up to the Palace steps she heard him barking in the hall, and exclaimed, 'There's Dash,' and was in a hurry to doff her crown and royal robe, and lay down the sceptre and the orb which she carried in her hand, and go and give Dash his bath." Leslie determined that should he live until another monarch came to the British throne he would not get up at three in the morning, and wait in the Abbey, attired in Court dress, till five in the afternoon, to see the Coronation ceremony.

The Queen had a hundred distinguished guests at her dinner-table that evening, and there was high festival throughout the land. The London theatres were open free; the whole town was illuminated, and there were grand displays of fireworks in the parks. There was feasting at

workhouses and hospitals and charity schools, and
in Hyde Park there was a Fancy Fair which lasted
four days. There was merrymaking all over the
country, and amongst English residents all over the
world. The total expense of the Coronation, so far
as the public purse was concerned, was £69,000,
and considering all things, it was cheaply done,
for the Coronation of George IV. cost the nation no
less than £238,000, even after Parliament had settled
that £100,000, was the amount to be expended.

A few months after the Coronation, Leslie was
at Windsor painting the portrait of the Queen,
who had given him sittings for the purpose of
his Coronation picture, which was afterwards
purchased by Her Majesty. When the Queen had
sat five times, Leslie writes : " She is so far satisfied
with the likeness that she does not wish me to
touch it again. She sat not only for the face, but
for as much as is seen of the figure, and for the
hands with the Coronation ring on the finger.
Her hands, by-the-bye, are very pretty, the backs
dimpled, and the fingers delicately shaped. She
was particular also in having her hair dressed
exactly as she wore it at the ceremony, every time
she sat." There were many portraits to introduce
in this painting, and for these it was necessary
that the distinguished personages should also give
Leslie sittings. Amongst others were the Dukes
of Cambridge, Sussex, and Wellington. These, in
one way or another, tried the artist very much, and
made him anxious to get back to his own home.

The Duke of Cambridge was usually silent, but when he did speak it was to ask a string of silly and tiresome questions. Sussex failed to keep his appointments and wasted three days of the artist's time, whilst Wellington annoyed Leslie by talking on matters of which he was ignorant. "You have made my head too large," said he, "and this is what all the painters have done to whom I have sat. Painters are not aware how small a part of the human figure the head is. Titian was the only painter who understood this, and by making the heads small he did wonders."

PRINCE ALBERT.

H.R.H ALBERT EDWARD, PRINCE OF WALES.

[To face Chap. VI.

ETON COLLEGE.

CHAPTER VI.
COURTSHIP AND WEDDING.

QUADRANGLE, ETON.

PRINCE ALBERT of Saxe-Coburg had written a nice cousinly letter to Queen Victoria congratulating her on becoming " Queen of the mightiest land in Europe," and hoping that she would still sometimes think of her cousins at Bonn. In October, 1839, King Leopold thought it was time to push forward the match that he had set his heart upon, and so he sent the brothers, Albert and Ernest, on a visit to Windsor. Their royal cousin received them with all honour, but their luggage had unfortunately gone astray,

F

and so they could not come into dinner with her the first day. But they joined the evening circle in their travelling clothes, and now began a very happy week. Every day the Princes rode with the Queen and a large cavalcade, and afterwards there was a grand dinner and three times a week a dance. It speedily became evident that the names of Victoria and Albert were to be linked together. The Prince was never willingly absent from her society, and strove to anticipate all her wishes. The Queen's mind was soon made up, and in her exalted position it was her place to "pop the question." One evening at a ball, after a dance with the young Prince, the Queen gave him her bouquet. The Prince was in uniform close buttoned to the throat, but he at once took out his penknife, cut a slit in the coat just over his heart, and safely placed the flowers there. On the following day the Queen sent for Prince Albert and made the offer, which he was only too glad to accept, and they were both very happy. Leopold was delighted at the news, and wrote, "May Albert be able to strew roses without thorns on the pathway of life of our good Victoria !"

The young Princes went back to Germany for a time, and the Queen had now to tell her Ministers and her Council what she intended to do. When the coming event was announced in the newspapers the people were very glad, and unmistakably showed their approbation when the Queen went to open Parliament in January, 1840, and to ask the Commons to vote an income for her husband.

On February 4th, Albert was brought in State to Buckingham Palace, where his intended bride and her mother met him at the door. The wedding took place on February 10th in the Chapel Royal of St. James's Palace. Out in the cold and rain stood thousands of spectators, who with "tremendous shouts" greeted the Queen as she drove through the crowded streets. " She was extremely pale," says Mrs. Oliphant, " as she passed along under the gaze of multitudes, her mother by her side, crowned with nothing but those pure flowers which are dedicated to the day of bridal, and not even permitted the luxury of a veil over her drooping face. The lace fell about her, but left her royal countenance unveiled. Even at that moment she belonged to her kingdom."

We need not linger over the wedding ceremony. We will just note that the royal bride was attired in white satin and orange-blossoms and a magnificent veil of Honiton lace. There were twelve noble maidens as bridesmaids, all in white satin and white roses. The chapel, sumptuously adorned for the occasion, was, of course, crowded with English nobility, foreign ambassadors, and so forth.

The Queen returned to the Palace no longer pale, but "with a joyous and open countenance, flushed, perhaps, in the slightest degree," and smiled to her applauding subjects. The sun shone out and there was real Queen's weather the rest of the day. After the wedding-breakfast was over, the young couple drove down to Windsor in a carriage and four, through twenty-two miles of spectators and innumerable "V.'s" and "A.'s" and other decorations. The Queen was now in a white satin pelisse profusely trimmed with swansdown, and there were white plumes over her white bonnet. The Prince was in a fur-trimmed coat with a high collar, and he had a high hat, which was in his hand nearly all the journey in response to the continuous salutations of the multitude. "Our reception," the Queen writes, "was most enthusiastic, hearty, and gratifying in every way, the people quite deafening us with their cheers— horsemen, etc., going along with us." All Windsor was sparkling with lights when they reached the town; and the Eton boys, the Queen tells us, "accompanied the carriage to the Castle, cheering and shouting as only schoolboys can. They swarmed up the mound as the carriage entered the Quadrangle; they made the old Castle ring again with their acclamations."

Not only in London, but all over England, people of all ranks held high festival on the occasion of the wedding of Queen Victoria to Prince Albert. Everybody seemed to approve the choice that had been made, and to be eager to join in the universal chorus of good wishes for the welfare of the young couple. In the grand banquetting room of St. James a very august company assembled. The Ministers of State gave grand dinners at their official residences. At the theatres all who chose to come were that evening admitted free, and when the orchestras played the National Anthem the crowded audiences stood up and showed their loyalty by deafening applause. At Drury Lane there was a special entertainment in honour of the occasion. It was something like a revival of one of those old masques that were so popular in England in the olden time. At the conclusion of the performance a representation of the Queen and Prince was seen surrounded by a grand display of fireworks, whereat all the liege subjects present were no doubt intensely gratified.

A few days after the wedding, in writing to her friend, Stockmar, the Queen says : " There cannot exist a purer, dearer, nobler being in the world than the Prince." The royal pair were soon back in London, and a very gay season of feasting and dancing and so on set in. Then there were Courts to be held and addresses almost numberless to be received. In one day Prince Albert received and answered twenty-seven addresses.

There is one important thing I have forgotten to mention—the Queen's wedding cake. It was three hundred pounds in weight, three yards in circumference, and fourteen inches in depth. On the top was Britannia blessing the royal couple, and amongst the other ornaments there was a Cupid writing in a volume spread open on his knees, " 10th of February, 1840 ; " there were, of course, plenty of flowers and lovers' knots and the usual decorations.

Prince Albert's father returned to Coburg a fortnight after the wedding. Notwithstanding the son's bright and happy prospects, the final parting was a time of deep feeling. " He told me, " writes the Queen, of Prince Albert, " that I had never known a father and could not therefore feel what he did. His childhood had been very happy. Ernest, he said, was now the only one remaining here of all his earliest ties and recollections ; but if I continued to love him as I did now I could make up for all. . . . Oh, how I did feel for my dear precious husband at that moment. Father, brother, friends, country, all has he left and all for me. God grant that I may be the happy person, the *most* happy person, to make this dearest blessed being happy and contented. What is in my power to make him happy I will do."

H.R.H. PRINCESS ALICE. [*To face Chap. VII.*

CHAPTER VII.

HOME LIFE.

WITHOUT a husband at her side, the young Queen had been liable to many worries and vexations from which she was now protected. A time of happiness and contentment set in. The Prince made it his great aim to be of as much use to Victoria as possible, and all the cares of State were lightened by his helpful companionship.

One of the early duties of the Prince was to reform the Palace arrangements, which were in strange confusion. Thus one part of the Palace was in charge of the Lord Steward, another part under the Lord Chamberlain, whilst for some other part no one was quite sure who was responsible. The Lord Chamberlain was responsible for cleaning the inside of the windows, the Commissioners of Woods and Forests the outsides. For providing fuel and laying fires the Lord Steward was responsible, for lighting them the Lord Chamberlain. So also providing lamps was under a different department from trimming and lighting them. "Before a pane of glass or a cupboard door could be mended," writes Stockmar, "the sanction of so many officials had to be obtained that often months elapsed before the repairs were made." Most of the servants were only responsible to some State official who did not reside in the Palace, and so they absented themselves when they pleased, and were guilty of all sorts of irregularities. But the Prince, by his wise tact, gradually set all these matters right.

The career of Prince Albert was providentially saved from being cut short by an accident during the first year of his married life. He was about to join a stag hunt on Ascot Heath when the Queen, who was going to follow in a pony phaeton, saw from one of the windows of Windsor Castle her husband cantering past on an excited horse. She watched the Prince as he struggled with his steed and managed to turn it round two or three times, and then the animal got the bit between his teeth and dashed off amongst the Park trees at the top

THE THAMES, FROM WINDSOR CASTLE.

of his speed. Prince Albert was brushed against a branch and swept off to the ground, but happily escaped without serious injury. A messenger was sent to assure the Queen of his safety, and the Prince mounted a fresh horse and went to the hunt. where Her Majesty soon joined him. The Queen thus writes in her journal: "Albert received me on the terrace of the large stand and led me up. He looked very pale and said he had been much alarmed lest I should have been frightened by his accident. . . . He told me he had scraped the skin off his poor arm, had bruised his hip and knee, and his coat was torn and dirty. It was a frightful fall."

The young pair were not only happy in their mutual love, but also in the similarity of their tastes. They sang and played together, drew and painted together; but a short extract from the Queen's book will best show how a day was spent at this period. "They breakfasted at nine, and took a walk every morning soon afterwards. Then came the usual amount of business (far less heavy, however, than now), besides which they drew and etched a great deal together, which was a source of great amusement, having the plates 'bit' in the house. Luncheon followed at the usual hour of two o'clock. Lord Melbourne (the Prime Minister at the time), came to the Queen in the afternoon, and between five and six the Prince generally drove her out in a pony phaeton. If the Prince did not drive the Queen, he rode; in which case she took a drive with the Duchess of Kent or the ladies. The Prince also read aloud most days to the Queen. The dinner was at eight o'clock, and always with the company. . . . The hours were never late, and it was very seldom that the party had not broken up at eleven o'clock." Of course there were exceptions to this rule, for the Queen gave many dinners, followed by dances. Lady Bloomfield (who was a maid of honour for some time) tells us how, "One lovely summer's morning —we had danced till dawn, and the Quadrangle being then open to the east—Her Majesty went out on the roof of the portico to see the sun rise, which was one of the most beautiful sights I ever remember. It rose behind St. Paul's, which we saw quite distinctly. Westminster Abbey, and the trees in the Green Park, stood out against a golden sky."

But duties were faithfully discharged, both by the Queen and her consort, amidst all this youthful gaiety. The Prince soon came out as an art patron, and on June 1st identified himself with the advocates of progress and philanthropy by taking the chair at a meeting for the abolition of the slave trade, and making his first speech in English. Caroline Fox, a young Quaker lady who was present, writes in her *Memories:* "The acclamations that attended the Prince's entrance were perfectly deafening, and he bore them all with calm, modest dignity, repeatedly bowing with considerable grace. He certainly is a very beautiful young man ; a thorough German, and a fine poetic specimen of the race. He uttered his speech in rather a low tone, and with the prettiest foreign accent."

From nature Sept:19. 1840—   *—. Eos*

ETCHINGS BY THE QUEEN, 1840.

We have referred to the Queen's exercise of her art talent by etching, and we are enabled to give four specimens of Her Majesty's work in this line, and at the head of this chapter is a single sample of the Prince's skill in the same field. As a young child the Queen had been taught drawing, and soon developed a love of art for its own sake. Throughout her journals there are many such entries as these: "We sat down on the ground, and Lady Canning and I sketched;" (when Prince Albert had shot a stag) "I sat down and scratched a little sketch of him on a bit of paper which I put on a stone."

There had been a great deal of absurd nonsense spoken and written about the place that the Prince should take on State occasions. Old-fashioned sticklers wanted to make out that the Queen's uncles, Sussex and Cambridge, were higher in rank than the Queen's husband. But the Prince soon lived down all this trumpery opposition, and the Duke of Wellington said, "Let the Queen put the Prince where she likes, and settle it herself, that is the best way." The Iron Duke's remark was equally to the purpose when Lord Albemarle, Master of the Horse, was tenaciously asserting his right to sit in the Sovereign's coach on State occasions. "The Queen," said Wellington, "can make Lord Albemarle sit at the top of the coach, under the coach, behind the coach, or wherever else Her Majesty pleases."

Before we turn to scenes of a more public

character, a little incident may be mentioned
connected with the early visits of the Queen and
Prince Albert to Claremont, a place associated with
so many fond memories and associations.   During
one of their rambles the royal couple were caught
in a shower and took refuge in a cottage.   The old
woman who dwelt there knowing nothing of the
high rank of her visitors, told them many remarkable stories about Princess Charlotte and Prince
Leopold.   At last the old lady offered to lend them
an umbrella.   But she was careful of her property
and made the Prince promise two or three times to
take great care of it and return it soon.   You may
imagine the old dame's surprise when she afterwards discovered with whom it was she had been
gossiping so freely.

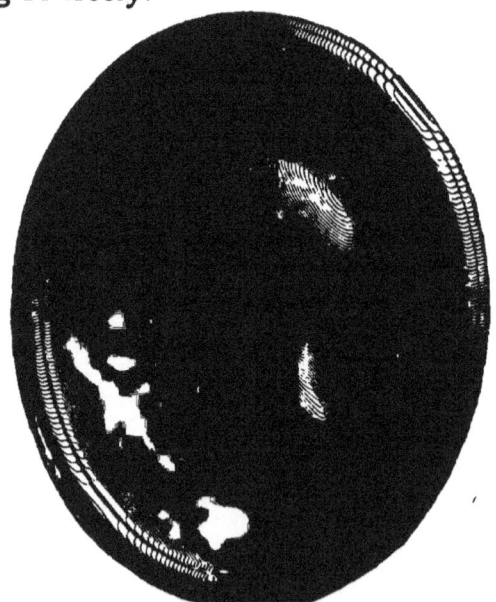

THE PRINCE CONSORT.

H.R.H. PRINCE ALFRED ERNEST, DUKE OF EDINBURGH.

[*To face Chap. VIII.*

CHAPTER VIII.

ATTEMPTS ON THE QUEEN'S LIFE.

IT seems strange that the life of a monarch so deservedly popular should have been so often attempted, yet it is the fact that Queen Victoria has been several times shot at. It is a comfort to think that in most cases a mere mad love of notoriety or downright insanity has prompted the attack.

In June, 1840, there was great distress throughout the country, the Ministry was unpopular, and severe things were being said in some of the newspapers about the Court festivities. The Queen was occasionally received by her subjects in silence, and on one or two occasions unpleasant and ominous shouts were heard. Much anxiety was being felt as regards the state of the nation, when suddenly it seemed as if a thrill of indignant horror passed through the land, as the news spread that the young Queen had been fired at, on Constitution Hill, on June 18th.

It was six o'clock on that summer's evening, and the Queen, as usual, was out driving with Prince Albert. A man leaning against the Park railing suddenly drew a pistol from his coat and fired at Her Majesty as she sat in the low open phaeton about six yards from him. The Queen was looking another way, and did not understand for a moment what had happened. The carriage stopped, but the Prince told the postillions to drive on. "I seized Victoria's hands," he wrote afterwards, "and asked if the fright had not shaken her, but she laughed." The Queen and Prince now both saw the man standing with a pistol in each hand, and almost immediately he fired again. Prince Albert drew the Queen down beside him, and the ball must have passed just over her head. A crowd gathered, and the man was seized; meanwhile, the Queen, after standing up once in the carriage to show that she was unhurt, drove rapidly to the house of the Duchess of Kent, to be the first to tell the news before any exaggerated reports reached her mother's ears. Then the royal pair returned to

Hyde Park ; the crowds of people on the footpaths, in the carriages, and on horseback, received them with enthusiastic cheers. All the riders from Rotten Row, ladies and gentlemen, escorted the Queen and Prince that day back to Buckingham Palace. The Queen, pale, but smiling and bowing, kept up bravely till she reached her own room, and then burst into tears. For several days afterwards a similarly large volunteer body-guard escorted her from the Park to the Palace gates. At all the theatres, "God Save the Queen" was sung with enthusiasm ; and at her first appearance at the Opera after the incident the tempest of loyal cheering and waving of handkerchiefs was beyond all precedent. The Lords and Commons, in full dress, came up to the Palace in a procession of about two hundred carriages, and presented an address of congratulation, which the Queen received sitting on her throne in state.

The wretched lad, Edward Oxford, whose failure was the cause of all this joy and thankfulness, was a discharged barman. It was proved that he came of a crazy family; and though the alarmists wanted to make out that he was one of a secret society pledged to treasonable practices, he was simply treated as a madman, and confined in Bedlam Thence he was sent to Dartmoor, and ultimately released on his promise to go to Australia, where he was working as a house-painter as lately as 1882. His conduct in prison was good, and he always declared that his attack on the

F

Queen was done out of sheer vanity and love of notoriety.

Having spoken of Oxford, we may as well refer to the other intrusions and attacks to which Her Majesty has been subjected, and so get done with the topic once for all. Our next instance is that of a very impudent, but comparatively harmless offender, known as "the boy Jones," who, in the course of two years, got four times into Buckingham Palace, and concealed himself behind furniture or up the chimney in the daytime. At night he supplied his wants in the kitchens, and curled himself up in some bed in a spare room. Very much astonished were the Palace servants at the sooty marks found in these beds when they were required. He boasted of having heard a long conversation between the Queen and the Prince whilst he was secreted behind a sofa. He was sentenced to three months in the House of Correction as a rogue and vagabond. On being liberated he took to haunting the outside of the Palace and the Parks when the Queen was driving. At length he was induced to go to sea, and is said to have died a well-to-do man in one of the Colonies.

On the 30th of May, 1842, the Queen was fired at for the second time. As she and the Prince were returning home from the Chapel Royal on the previous day (Sunday), the Prince had seen a man step out and present a pistol, which missed fire. A boy came to the Palace in the afternoon and described the same incident, which had been seen apparently by no one else. The Queen and Prince resolved to go out next day as usual, though both were much agitated, and the Queen was far from well. Her Majesty, however, would not allow any of her ladies to accompany her, as was customary. The royal pair were returning from their drive, and had nearly reached the scene of Oxford's attempt two years before, when " a little, swarthy, ill-looking rascal," whom the Prince recognised as the would-be assailant of the day before, fired at the Queen, a shot which passed harmlessly by. The man was secured by a policeman. As for the royal couple—" We felt as if a load had been taken off our hearts," wrote the Prince, " and we thanked the Almighty for having preserved us a second time from so great a danger."

Joyful shouts again greeted the Queen's public appearance after this escape from danger. John Francis, the assailant, was sentenced to death, a sentence, however, which was commuted (in full accordance with the Queen's anxious desires) to banishment for life. On Sunday, the 3rd of July, the day after the sentence of Francis had been commuted, the Queen, whilst returning by the side of her uncle, King Leopold, from the Chapel Royal, St. James's, was again in danger from a would-be assailant. This time it was a hunchback named Bean, whose pistol missed fire, but was found to be loaded with bits of tobacco pipe. He eluded capture at the moment, and for about a fortnight all the poor hunchbacks in London had a very bad time of it. They were hooted at and accused in the public streets, and had to be very ready with *alibis* for the particular afternoon referred to. At length, Bean was caught and sentenced to a term of imprisonment.

For seven years the Queen enjoyed an immunity from these attacks, till on May 19th, 1849, a man standing within the railings of the Green Park, fired at her as she was driving up Constitution Hill. Prince Albert was riding at some distance in front. The Queen did not lose her self-possession; she stood up a moment and bade the coachman (who had stopped) drive on, and then talked to her three children, who were with her, to divert their attention. The man, an Irishman, named Hamilton, was arrested, and subsequently sentenced (as his pistol contained no bullet) to seven years' transportation.

In June, 1850, Her Majesty was the victim of an outrage of another character—one of the most wanton and cowardly of the whole series of attacks to which she has been subjected. She was returning from a visit to her uncle, the Duke of Cambridge, then suffering from his last illness. Beside the entrance of Cambridge House, a tall gentlemanly man was loitering as if waiting to get a sight of the Queen. As her carriage drove out of the gateway and was turning the corner into the road, this man rushed forward and struck the Queen a sharp blow on the face with a small stick. Her Majesty's bonnet was crushed by the blow, and a severe bruise and slight wound were inflicted on her forehead. The perpetrator of this cruel act soon found himself in the police station. He was a man of thirty, a gentleman by birth and education, but evidently not of sound mind. He was well known for conspicuous conduct in the Park, and his eccentricities had lost him his position as an officer in the army. He was now sentenced to seven years' transportation. The Queen was well enough to be at the Opera on the evening after the assault, and was joyfully received.

In February, 1872, when about to alight from her carriage after a drive, a youth rushed at the Queen with a paper in one hand and a pistol in the other. The Queen's attendant, John Brown, seized the lad, who as usual, was found to be not quite right in his mind. Arthur O'Connor (for this was his name) was an Irish boy of about seventeen who had brooded over his country's wrongs till he fancied he could do some good by making Her Majesty read a petition he had drawn up on behalf of the Fenians. He had accordingly climbed over the railings to carry out the project which John Brown so promptly interrupted. But his damaged pistol was found to have no ball in it. Public indignation was strongly expressed on the occasion, and the culprit was soon put under care suited to his mental condition. The Queen had already been on the point of issuing medals to domestics who had served her long and faithfully, and so now John Brown had the first gold medal and an annuity of twenty-five pounds.

The last of these attacks took place only four years ago (in 1882) at Royal Windsor. The Queen, accompanied by the Princess Beatrice, was entering her carriage at Windsor station, when she was fired at by a man named Roderick Maclean, who was at once arrested. The prisoner, who had formerly been respectable, but had recently fallen into want, was tried for high treason. Being found not guilty, on the ground of insanity, he was ordered to be imprisoned during Her Majesty's pleasure.

VALE OF GLENCOE.

THE PRINCESS ROYAL AS A CHILD.

THE OLD PALACE OF BALMORAL.

CHAPTER IX.

ROYAL BABIES.

THE FIRST OF THE QUEEN'S BABIES.

THE first of the royal babies to put in an appearance was Victoria Adelaide Mary Louisa, the Princess Royal of England, now also Crown Princess of Germany, who was born at Buckingham Palace, on November 21st, 1840. Two days after the event, Mr. Selwyn came as usual to the Palace to read law with Prince Albert; but the Prince said, "I fear I cannot read any law to-day,

there are so many coming to congratulate, but
you will like to see the little Princess." He conducted Mr. Selwyn to the nursery, where the child
was sleeping. Then taking the baby's hand, the
Prince said, "The next time we read, it must be
on the rights and duties of a Princess Royal."

The christening took place on February 10th,
1841. On the day previous Prince Albert was
skating on the lake in Buckingham Palace
Gardens when he suddenly went through the ice
into deep water. The Queen came to the edge of
the ice and rendered such efficient aid that the
Prince scrambled out, whilst the lady-in-waiting
was "more occupied in screaming for help." A
bad cold was the worst result of this dangerous
accident that might so easily have had a fatal
termination.

The christening was performed, with all due
ceremony, by two archbishops, two bishops,
and a dean, in the presence of many noble personages. The new silver-gilt font was in the
shape of a water lily supporting a shell ; the water
used on the occasion had been brought from the
Jordan. In a letter to his grandmother, at Gotha,
Prince Albert says : "The christening went off
very well ; your little great granddaughter behaved
with great propriety, and like a Christian. She
was awake, but did not cry at all, and seemed to
crow with immense satisfaction at the lights and
brilliant uniforms, for she is very intelligent and
observing. The ceremony took place at half-past

six p.m. After it there was a dinner, and then we had some instrumental music."

— The Prince of Wales came to share the nursery with his sister on November 9th, 1841. The Lord Mayor's Show was setting out from Guildhall when the booming of the Tower guns announced the new arrival. The christening took place on January 25th, 1842. It was a time of trouble and unsettlement. From abroad the news had come of English soldiers perishing by thousands in the rugged defiles of Afghanistan ; at home there was great distress, vast numbers of workmen were only on half-time or out of work altogether, pauperism and crime had increased to an enormous extent. Mainly in consequence of the wicked bread tax, fearful evils had developed, which could only be remedied by the advent of Free Trade, which came five years later. Some of the newspapers took to printing statements respecting the Court festivities and the Queen's ball dresses, side by side with accounts of deaths from starvation and similar horrors. Sir Robert Peel, who was now Prime Minister, advised a general limitation of costly display under existing circumstances, and the Queen, with characteristic good sense and good feeling, cordially endorsed her Minister's admonition. All the ladies present at the Royal christening wore only Paisley shawls, English lace, and other home manufactured goods ; and all through the season of 1842 a general soberness was manifest.

THE ROYAL CHILDREN (after Winterhalter's Painting).

Still, the christening of the Prince of Wales was celebrated with due splendour in St. George's Chapel, Windsor. The child (as everyone knows) was christened Albert Edward, and the *Times* says he "behaved with princely decorum."

During the summer of 1842, in spite of general anxiety, dinners, concerts, and balls were fully encouraged for the promotion of trade. One famous ball has never been forgotten by those who took part in it. This was the "Queen's Plantagenet Ball," when, for one evening, Buckingham Palace wore the aspect of the Court of Edward III. and Queen Philippa. In the preparations for this ball, it was said that eighteen thousand persons were more or less employed. Her Majesty, as Queen Philippa, wore a dress entirely made in Spitalfields. Prince Albert represented Edward III. It is not needful to enumerate the characters personated by the crowd of nobles who were present, but the whole affair was acknowledged to be the most splendid *fête* of the reign.

The Queen received visits from eminent persons at various times in a quiet way. Mendelssohn, the great composer, was twice at the Palace this summer. The Queen and Prince were delighted with his performances ; and Mendelssohn was also delighted to hear them play and sing, and astonished at their proficiency.

As this chapter is mainly about these first royal babies, let us glance at their infancy before talking of other topics. Referring to one occasion when she was obliged to keep her bed, in November, 1841, the Queen writes : "Albert brought in dearest little Pussy (the Princess Royal) in such a smart white merino frock trimmed with blue, which mamma had given her, and a pretty cap, and placed her on my bed, seating himself next to her, and she was very dear and good. And as my precious invaluable Albert sat there, and our little love between us, I felt quite moved with happiness and gratitude to God."

"When the youthful pair were a little older," says Miss Tytler, " they would stand still and quiet in the music room to hear the Prince-father discourse sweet sounds on his organ and the Queen-mother sing with one of her ladies. . . . The small people furnished a never-ending series of merry anecdotes. . . . Now it was the little princess, a quaint tiny figure in ' dark blue velvet and white shoes and yellow kid gloves' keeping the nurseries alive with her sports, showing off the new frocks she had got as a Christmas-box from her grand-mamma, the Duchess of Kent, and bidding Miss Liddell put one on. Now it was the Queen offending the dignity of her little daughter by calling her ' Missy,' and being told in indignant tones ' I am not Missy, I'm the Princess Royal.' Or it was Lady Lyttelton, who was warned off by the dismissal in French from the morsel of royalty, not quite three, ' N'approchez pas moi, moi ne veut pas vous.' "

H.R.H. PRINCESS HELENA (PRINCESS CHRISTIAN) AND HER DAUGHTER.

From Photograph by Messrs. Downey.]   [*To face Chap. X.*

CHAPTER X.

VISITS TO SCOTLAND AND FRANCE.

DALKEITH.

IN the Autumn of 1842, the Queen paid her first visit to Scotland. The royal yacht carried her to Leith Roads, and at eight the following morning she landed and proceeded to Edinburgh. The good people of the city, who had been very busy all the day before over their preparations, and had been waiting in thousands for her arrival, did not now expect her till the middle of the day. The watchers who should have signalled her approach blundered over it, and so the Lord Provost and Corporation, who meant to have received her at the gates with all due ancient ceremonies, were suddenly astonished to hear that the Queen was passing through the city. She went to the Duke of Buccleugh's Palace at Dalkeith, and rested there till Saturday, and then visited Edinburgh in State. The disappointed Provost and his Baillies gave her the town keys, and she very graciously handed them back again. On through the densely crowded and gaily decorated streets the Queen came, wearing the Royal Stuart tartan and greeted with loud acclamations. Through old historic streets, and past old historic buildings, famous in song and story, she drove on to the lordly castle whose ramparts were scaled by Black Douglas. They showed her all that was noteworthy in that celebrated fortress, but most of all the Queen admired the splendid view from the ramparts—the cld town at her feet, the rich Lothians, the gleaming Frith, and blue mountains far away.

From Edinburgh the Queen travelled to the Highlands, and everywhere realised a true " Highland Welcome." Triumphal arches sprang up at her approach. There were gatherings of clans, balls, deerstalking, processions of boats, and all sorts of attractions and entertainments. At Taymouth, the seat of the Marquis of Breadalbane, there was a grand reception, which is thus described by Her Majesty: " The *coup d'œil* was indescribable. There were a number of Lord Breadalbane's highlanders, all in the Campbell tartan, drawn up in front of the house, with Lord Breadalbane, himself in a Highland dress, at their head; a few of Sir Niel Menzies' men (in the Menzies' red and white tartan), a number of pipers playing, and a company of the 92nd Highlanders, also in kilts. The firing of the guns, the cheering of the great crowd, the picturesqueness of the dresses, the beauty of the surrounding country, with its rich background of wooded hills, altogether formed one of the finest scenes imaginable. It seemed as if a great chieftain in olden feudal times was receiving his Sovereign. It was princely and romantic."

The tour only lasted a fortnight—in the course of it no less than 656 post-horses were employed—and then the Queen and Prince returned to London.

In August, 1843, the Queen and Prince Albert made a yachting excursion about the South Coast, in the course of which a curious little incident occurred. The Queen landed at Southampton when it was raining heavily, and the landing stage was not properly covered. But everyone who has heard of Queen Elizabeth and Sir Walter Raleigh knows what is proper to be done on such an occasion, and the members of the Corporation at once pulled off their red gowns and spread them on the pier to make a dry footway for their Queen. The Cambridge students enacted a similar performance a few months afterwards.

The next cruise of the Queen and Prince was to France—the first visit of an English Sovereign to that country since Henry VIII. and Francis I. met

G

on the Field of the Cloth of Gold. Louis Philippe, the Citizen King, "stout, florid, and bluff-looking, with thick, grizzled hair, brushed up into a point," and Queen Amelie, "with her snowy curls and benevolent face," met the Queen at Treport and escorted her to the Royal Chateau. One account says that Louis Philippe came on board the yacht, caught up the little Queen of England, kissed her on both cheeks, and carried her bodily on to his barge. The visit altogether seems to have been a very pleasurable time.

The Queen's next visit was to see her uncle and aunt at Brussels. "Little Charlotte," three years old, is spoken of in a letter as "quite the prettiest child you ever saw." That little Charlotte is now the widowed ex-Empress of Mexico, pining in melancholy madness in her sad retreat.

Czar Nicholas, of Russia, who came to the Palace in 1844, impressed everyone by his manly dignity and polished courtesy. He gave magnificent presents of jewels to the Court ladies, and was altogether very popular. In September, about a month after the birth of Prince Alfred, the Queen paid her second visit to the Highlands and took her little four year old daughter with her. The royal party went to Lord Glenlyon's seat at Blair Athol. Here State and ceremony were as much as possible dispensed with, and the royal pair and their little one thoroughly enjoyed a simple and retired life. The Queen was roused at dawn by a Highland piper beneath her window,

and was speedily about the grounds with the
Prince. One morning a plainly-dressed lady left
the castle alone. Presently it seemed to have
struck one of the Highland guard on duty that it
must have been the Queen. A party of Highlanders forthwith hurried after the lady as a
body-guard, but she sent them home again. The
Queen, wishing to arrange about a projected
excursion to the Falls of Bruar, wandered through
the grounds to the lodge where Lord and Lady
Glenlyon were temporarily residing. His lordship
was, however, not up, and the servant, when told
to say that the Queen had called, was astounded.
Her Majesty tried to return by a different route
and lost her way. She had to ask some reapers in
an oatfield, who pointed out her route across a
field and over some palings beyond. The Queen
followed their instructions and climbed the
palings, and found herself in the Castle grounds
once more.

During this enjoyable excursion the Princess
Royal often rode on a little Shetland pony beside
her parents. Her father wrote, " Pussy's cheeks
are ón the point of bursting, they have grown so
red and plump. She is learning Gaelic, but makes
wild work of the names of the mountains."

On one occasion the Queen and Prince went on
ponies, accompanied by one attendant, Sandy
McAra, to the top of the hill of Tulloch, and
enjoyed the grand mountain panorama from the
summit. " It was quite romantic," writes the

Queen. "Here we were, with only the Highlander behind us holding the ponies—for we got off twice and walked about; not a house, not a creature near us, but the pretty Highland sheep, with their horns and black faces, up at the top of Tulloch, surrounded by beautiful mountains . . . the most delightful, the most romantic ride I ever had." Upon her Highland pony the Queen took many a ride amongst the forests and mountains, joyfully exploring the scenery of romantic glens seldom seen by visitors. But sightseers did find their way even to this secluded region, and would throng the little church at Blair Athol for the chance of watching royalty worshipping.

LOUIS PHILIPPE.

H.R.H. PRINCESS LOUISE, MARCHIONESS OF LORNE.

[To face Chap. XI.

CHAPTER XI.

STATE CEREMONIES AND FESTIVITIES.

ROYAL EXCHANGE.

THE Queen and Prince Albert returned to Windsor to receive Louis Philippe on the occasion of the first voluntary visit of the King of France to the English Court. The King was delighted with everything, and amidst all that grandeur and festivity enjoyed chatting with the Queen about the experiences of his youth in exile—for instance, when he was a teacher in Switzerland earning twenty pence a day and cleaning his own boots. The King was duly entertained with banquets and festivities, and made a Knight of the Garter. His Minister, Guizot, accompanied him; and in his *Memoirs* he tells us how one night on retiring to his room he lost his way, and appeared to wander along miles of corridors and stairs. At last, believing he recognised the room door, he turned the handle, but immediately withdrew, on getting a glimpse of a lady sitting at a toilet table, with a maid busy about her mistresses hair. It was not till next day, from some smiling words addressed to him by the Queen, the horrified statesman discovered he had been guilty of an invasion of the royal apartments."

In October of this year there were grand doings in London on the occasion of the opening of the New Royal Exchange. The Queen, in white satin and silver tissue and sparkling with jewels, came in her State carriage with the cream-coloured horses through the streets, where her subjects in countless thousands assembled to greet her. At Temple Bar the Corporation of London were waiting. in State to receive their liege lady—the Aldermen in scarlet robes,the Common Councilmen in blue cloaks, the Lord Mayor gorgeously arrayed in a robe of crimson velvet, a collar of S.S., and a Spanish hat and feather! But over his shoes and stockings the cautious Lord Mayor had drawn on a pair of jack-boots to keep.the mud off his silk-clad calves till the right moment. The signal was given that the Queen was coming, but unfortunately the boots were too tight and wouldn't come off at once as intended. In his nervous efforts the Lord Mayor caught one of his spurs in the fur of an alderman's robe, and this of course produced more confusion. The Lord Mayor was standing with one boot off and with several men tugging at the other one. The Queen's carriage came nearer and nearer,

and his lordship's agonies and fever of anxiety
increased till at length he cried wildly to the men,
with a spice of strong language, to have that other
boot pulled on again.

He was only just in time to step forward in his
muddy jack-boots and bow to Her Majesty. He
offered her the City sword, which she touched in
sign of acceptance, and then waved back. As for
the poor Lord Mayor he had to wear those horrible
boots until the banquet, and only just managed to
get rid of them before sitting down to table.

The royal procession swept through the City
to the Exchange. The first Royal Exchange, built
by Sir Thomas Gresham, was opened by Queen
Elizabeth and destroyed in the Great Fire of
London. The next was burnt down in 1838, and
replaced by the present noble edifice. On the
occasion we are now referring to the Queen made
the tour of the building, received an address, gave
the Lord Mayor her hand to kiss and promised to
make him a baronet, and then partook, in company
with an assemblage of noble and distinguished
persons, of a grand banquet in the great room of the
underwriters, ninety-eight feet long by forty wide.
At two o'clock all assembled in the great central
quadrangle, the heralds proclaimed silence, and the
Queen, standing on the spot where her statue now
stands, declared "It is my royal will and pleasure
that this building be hereafter called 'The Royal
Exchange.'" The royal party then went home,
but at the Mansion House and the halls of the

Livery Companies, festivities were kept up that night to a very late hour.

At the close of 1844 and beginning of 1845 the Queen was engaged in a royal progress to the

INNER COURT, BURGHLEY HOUSE.

houses of some of her nobility. She went to Burghley, the seat of the Marquis of Exeter, and in

so doing trod in the footsteps of Queen Elizabeth.
Queen Victoria attended as godmother the christening of an infant child of the marquis; the little
girl was named "Lady Victoria Cecil." Early in
the new year the Queen and Prince Albert went to
Stowe, the grand palace of the Duke of Buckingham. This visit became almost notorious for the
tremendous slaughter of hares and pheasants
by the gentlemen of the party. After a short
return to Windsor, the Queen visited the Duke of
Wellington at Strathfieldsaye. This visit had
more of a private and friendly character than is
usual in visits of Sovereigns to their subjects.
"There was much that was unique and kindly,"
says Miss Tytler, "in the relations between the
Queen and the greatest soldier of the day. He had
stood by her baptismal font; she had been his
guest, when she was the girl-princess, at Walmer;
he had sat in her first council; she was to give his
name to one of her sons; in fact, he had taken part
in every event of her life. The present arrangements were a graceful, well-nigh filial tribute of
affectionate regard for the old man who had served
his country both in the battle field and in the senate,
who had watched his Queen's career with the
keenest interest, and rejoiced in her success as
something with which he had to do."

There was another great costume ball, which
became known as "The Powder Ball," at Buckingham Palace, in 1845. All the guests dressed in the
style of 1750, when hair powder was in fashion.

Miss Burdett-Coutts wore a diadem and necklace that had once belonged to Maria Antoinette.

In the Autumn of 1845, the Queen paid her first visit to Germany. At Bonn, she saw the "little house" where her husband and his brother lived whilst they were students at the University. At Coburg there was a hearty public reception. Rosenau was given up to them, and the Prince showed the Queen the room which he and his brother used to occupy when children. "It is quite in the roof," writes the Queen, "with a little tiny bedroom on each side, in one of which they both used to sleep with Florschutz, their tutor. The view is beautiful, and the paper is still full of holes from their fencing; and the very same table is there on which they were dressed when little."

They visited Gotha, where the Queen was rejoiced to meet her old governess, Baroness Lehzen. In the adjacent forest, a barbarous "deer drive" took place in the German fashion. About thirty stags and other animals were driven from the forest into an enclosure, before which sat the royal and noble guests in arm chairs. There was a band of music, and in the intervals between the pieces, the gentlemen loaded their rifles and fired at their prey. The ladies had to sit and look on, but the Queen says in her journal: "As for the sport itself, none of the gentlemen like this butchery." *Punch* smartly satirised the whole affair in a poem, entitled "The Sportsman of Gotha."

THE PRINCE OF WALES WHEN A BOY (*after Landseer*).

ABERDEEN.

CHAPTER XII.

ROYAL LIFE IN THE HIGHLANDS.

INVERARY CASTLE.

A BOOK, entitled *"Leaves from the Journal of Our Life in the Highlands,"* has been published by the Queen, giving details of many sojourns in Scotland after the purchase of Balmoral in 1848. The Queen had visited the West Coast of Scotland in 1847. At Inverary she saw a child "just two years old—a dear, white, fat, fair little fellow, with reddish hair but very delicate features, like both his mother and father; he is such a merry, independent little child. He had a black velvet dress and jacket, with a 'sporran' scarf and Highland bonnet." That child was the Marquis of Lorne—Her Majesty's son-in-law at a future date.

The Queen greatly enjoyed this excursion, during which she spent four weeks in the Highlands. On March 18th, 1848, the future wife of that little Marquis, at Inverary, was born and named Louise Caroline Alberta. In less than a fortnight afterwards, Princess Sophia, daughter of George III. and Queen Charlotte, died quietly in her arm chair, at Kensington, at the age of seventy-one.

In September, 1848, the Queen purchased for a royal residence the estate of Balmoral, on the banks of the Dee, in Aberdeenshire. The Queen thus describes her new abode : " We arrived at Balmoral at a quarter to three. It is a pretty little castle in the old Scottish style. There is a picturesque tower, and garden in front with a high wooded hill; at the back there is a wood down to the Dee, and the hills rise all around. . . . At half-past four we walked out and went up to the top of the wooded hill opposite our windows, where there is a cairn, and up which there is a pretty winding path. The view from here looking down upon the house is charming. To the left you look towards the beautiful hills surrounding Lochnagar, and to the right towards Ballater, to the glen along which the Dee winds with beautiful wooded hills. It was so calm and so solitary, it did one good as one gazed around; and the pure mountain air was most refreshing. All seemed to breathe freedom and peace."

In this charming home, or rather in the new castle-mansion built in its place, year after year the royal family resided at intervals, and enjoyed excursions, drives, Highland sports, deer-stalking, fishing, and *incognito* journeys of exploration. Many are the curious incidents recorded in the Queen's book, which gives Highland experiences up to 1861. On one occasion she says, "We then came to a place which is always wet, but was particularly bad after the late rain and snow. There was no pony for me to get on, and as I wished not to get my feet wet by walking through the long grass, Albert proposed that I should be carried over in a plaid; and Lenchen* was first carried over, but was held too low and her feet dangled; so Albert suggested that the plaid should be put round the men's shoulders and that I should sit upon it. Brown and Duncan, the two strongest and handiest, were the two who undertook it, and I sat safely enough with an arm on each man's shoulder and was carried success-fully over."

The following extract from the same book shows the Queen's interest in her poorer neighbours. In the secluded Highland valleys she could visit the poor in their own dwellings, and freely talk

---

* The Princess Helena.

to them and safely indulge her benevolent inclin-
ations.

"Albert went out with Alfred for the day, and
I walked out with the two girls and Lady
Churchill, stopped at the shop and made some
purchases for poor people and others; drove a
little way, got out and walked up the hill to
Balnacroft (Mrs. P. Farquharson's), and she
walked round with us to some of the cottages to
show me where the poor people lived and to tell
them who I was. Before we went into any, we
met an old woman, who, Mrs. Farquharson said,
was very poor, eighty-six years old, and mother
to the former distiller. I gave her a warm petticoat,
and the tears rolled down her old cheeks, and she
shook my hands and prayed God to bless me: it
was very touching.

"I went into a small cabin of old Kitty Kear's,
who is eighty-six years old, quite erect, and
welcomed us with a great air of dignity. She
sat down and spun. I gave her also a warm
petticoat; she said, 'May the Lord ever attend
you and yours, here and hereafter; and may the
Lord be a guide to ye and keep ye from all harm.'
She was quite surprised at Vicky's height; great
interest is taken in her. We went on to a cottage
to visit old widow Simmons, who is 'past four-
score,' with a nice rosy face, but was bent quite
double; she was most friendly, shaking hands
with us all, asking which was I, and repeating
many kind blessings.

"We went into three other cottages: to Mrs.
Symon's, who had an 'unwell boy;' then across
a little burn to another old woman's; and afterwards peeped into Blair the fiddler's. We drove
back and got out to see old Mrs. Grant, who is so
tidy and clean, and to whom I gave a dress and
handkerchief, and she said, 'You're too kind to
me, you're over kind to me, ye give me more every
year;—and I get older every year.'

"Really the affection of these poor people, who
are so hearty and happy to see you taking an
interest in everything, is very touching and
gratifying."

And now we will take a few peeps at the Queen
and royal family when engaged in one of the
incognito journeys we have alluded to. After
describing a morning walk from Balmoral, five
miles, to Geldie, and then a long ride on ponies
amongst wild hills and glens, she says: "We
came upon Lock Inch, which is lovely, and of
which I should have liked exceedingly to have
taken a sketch, but we were pressed for time and
hurried. . . . We parted from our ponies, only
Grant and Brown coming on with us. Walker,
the Police Inspector, met us, but did not keep
with us. He had been sent to order everything in
a quiet way, without letting people suspect who
we were. In this he entirely succeeded. The ferry
was a very rude affair, it was like a boat or cobble;
but we could only stand on it, and it was moved
at one end by two long oars, plied by the ferryman

H

and Brown, and at the other end by a long sort of beam, which Grant took in hand. A few seconds brought us over to the road, where there were two shabby vehicles, one, a kind of barouche, into which Albert and I got; Lady Churchill and General Grey into the other—a break; each with a pair of small and rather miserable horses, driven by a man from the box. Grant was on our carriage, and Brown on the other. We had gone, so far, forty miles; at least twenty on horseback. We had decided to call ourselves Lord and Lady Churchill and party, Lady Churchill passing as Miss Spencer, and General Grey as Dr. Grey. Brown once forgot this, and called out 'Your Majesty,' as I was getting into the carriage; and Grant, on the box, once called Albert ' Your Royal Highness,' which set us off laughing, but no one noticed it."

The Queen goes on to describe the almost perfect solitude of the journey and the gathering darkness. " At length we saw lights, and drove through a long and straggling 'town,' and turned down a small court to the door of the inn. Here we got out quickly, Lady Churchill and General Grey not waiting for us. We went up a small staircase and were shown to our bedroom at the top of it— very small, but clean—with a large four-post bed, which nearly filled the room. Opposite was the drawing and dining room in one, very tidy and well-sized. Then came the room where Albert dressed, which was very small. The two maids

(Jane Shackle was one), had driven over by another road in the waggonette, Stewart driving them. Made ourselves clean and tidy, and then sat down to our dinner. Grant and Brown were to have waited on us, but were bashful and did not. A ringletted woman did everything; and when dinner was over removed the cloth and placed the bottle of wine (our own which we had brought) on the table, with the glasses, which was the old English fashion. The dinner was very fair, and all very clean—soup, 'hodge podge,' mutton broth with vegetables (which I did not much relish), fowl with white sauce, good roast lamb, very good potatoes, besides one or two other dishes which I did not taste; ending with a good tart of cranberries. After dinner I tried to write part of this account (but the talking round me confused me), while Albert played at 'Patience.'"

Next morning, after a drive in the neighbour-hood, the party had to pass through Grantown (which was the name of the place) again, and now it was evident that people had got to know the truth. "All the people," says the Queen, "were now in the street, and the landlady waved her pocket handkerchief, and the ringletted maid (who had curl papers in the morning) waved a flag from the window. Our coachman evidently did not observe or guess anything."

A similar excursion, at another time, is referred to by the Queen as follows: "At a quarter-past seven o'clock we reached the small, quiet town, or rather village, of Fettercairn, for it was very small, —not a creature stirring, and we got out at the quiet little inn, ' Ramsay Arms,' quite unobserved, and went at once upstairs.   There was a very nice drawing-room, and next to it a dining-room, both very clean and tidy; then to the left our bedroom, which was excessively small, but also very clean and neat.   Alice had a nice room the same size as ours; then came a mere morsel of one in which Albert dressed; and then came Lady Churchill's bedroom just beyond.   Louis and General Grey had rooms in 'The Temperance Hotel,' opposite. We dined at eight—a very nice clean dinner. Grant and Brown waited; they were rather nervous; but General Grey and Lady Churchill carved, and they had only to change the plates, which Brown soon got into the way of doing.   A little girl of the house came in to help, but Grant turned her round to prevent her looking at us.   The landlord and landlady knew who we were, but no one else except the coachman, and they kept the secret admirably.

"The evening being bright and moonlight and very still, we all went out and walked through the whole village, where not a creature moved . . . . hearing nothing whatever but the distant barking of a dog.   Suddenly we heard a drum and fifes. We were greatly alarmed, fearing we had been recognised; but Louis and General Grey, who went back, saw nothing whatever.   Still, as we walked slowly back, we heard the noise from time to time—and when we reached the inn door we stopped, and saw six men march up with fifes and a drum (not a creature taking any notice of them), go down the street and back again. Grant and Brown were out, but had no idea what it could be. Albert asked the little maid, and the answer was, ' It's just a band,' and that it walked about in this way twice a week. How odd ! It went on playing some time after we got home. We sat till half-past ten working, and Albert reading—and then retired to rest."

Here is another scene, when a cairn was being raised on one of the heights near Balmoral, to celebrate the building of the new Castle. The Queen and Prince with the royal children, and the ladies and gentlemen staying at the Castle, went one fine morning to the top of Craig Cowan, where the children of the tenants and the Queen's servants were already assembled. The Queen laid the first stone, the Prince the second, and then each of the children, according to their ages. Then all the ladies and gentlemen of the Court placed a stone each. The pipers played merrily, and dancing and merry revels went on all round, until in the course of an hour the cairn was built. When the cairn was about eight feet high, and was thought to be nearly complete, Prince Albert climbed to the top and put the last stone in position, and with three hearty cheers from those assembled proceedings terminated. The Queen says, in con-cluding her narrative of the transaction : " It was a gay, pretty and touching sight, and I felt almost inclined to cry. The view was so beautiful over the dear hills, the day so fine, the whole so *gemüthlich*. May God bless this place, and allow us yet to see it and enjoy it many a long year."'

BALMORAL—THE NEW CASTLE.

At another page of her book, the Queen writes concerning Balmoral: "Every year my heart becomes more fixed in this dear Paradise, and so much more now, that *all* has become my dearest Albert's *own* creation, own work, own building, own laying out, as at Osborne; and his great taste, and the impress of his dear hand, have been stamped everywhere. He was very busy to-day, settling and arranging many things for next year."

Some people might, perhaps, be disappointed at finding in the Queen's simple diary so little reference to Court splendour, or to rank and ancestry, and all that sort of thing. But this is really the great charm of the volume. Crown and sceptre are left out of sight, and the true woman reveals herself on every page. Almost the only reference to her rank is found where she records : "It was the first time the British standard with the Queen of Great Britain and her husband and children had ever entered Fingal's Cave." The relics at Perth and at Holyrood, associated with the misfortunes of her royal ancestors, did not cause her much personal emotion, but on passing the Farne Islands she makes the entry, "We were very sorry to hear that poor Grace Darling had died the night before."

One more brief extract from this fascinating volume, and then we must leave our young readers to read it all through themselves, when they get the opportunity. The Queen and Prince " highly appreciated the good breeding, simplicity and intelligence" of the Highlanders, and liked to converse with them. " Albert went on further with the children," says the Queen, referring to a mountain excursion to the source of the Dee, " but I returned with Grant to my seat, as I could not scramble about well. I and Alice rode part of the

way, walking wherever it was very steep. Albert
and Bertie walked the whole time, Albert talking
so gaily with Grant.   Upon which Brown observed
to me in simple Highland phrase : 'It's very
pleasant to walk with a person who is always
content.'   Yesterday, in speaking of dear Albert's
sport, when I observed he never was cross after
bad luck, Brown said : ' Everyone on the estate
says there never was so kind a master ; I am sure
our only wish is to give satisfaction.'   I said they
certainly did."

THE PRINCE CONSORT, 1860.

OSBORNE HOUSE.

OLD WEIR BRIDGE, LAKE OF KILLARNEY.

CHAPTER XIII.

THE QUEEN IN IRELAND.

DUBLIN CASTLE.

THE Queen paid her first visit to Ireland in the autumn of 1849. She arrived in the "Fairy" at the Cove of Cork whilst bonfires blazed upon the neighbouring hills, and rockets shot up from the ships in the harbour. Next day the "Fairy" steamed round the harbour and then lay beside the pier at Cove to receive various deputations with addresses, "after which," says the Queen, "to give the people the satisfaction of calling the place 'Queenstown,' in honour of its being the first spot on which I set foot upon Irish ground, I stepped on shore amid the roar of cannon (for the artillery was placed so close as quite to shake the temporary room into which we entered) and the enthusiastic shouts of the people."

At Cork itself there were more addresses, and a splendid reception. The Queen rode through Cork in Lord Bandon's carriage, and so many carriages and horsemen joined the procession that it took two

TRIUMPHAL ARCH, PATRICK STREET, CORK.

hours to pass through the crowded streets. The Queen took much notice of the good-humoured, noisy crowd; the men, often raggedly dressed in their blue coats and knee-breeches and blue stockings, the women, in their long blue cloaks, and "with such dark eyes and hair, and such fine teeth; almost every third woman was pretty, and some remarkably so." The four royal children pleased the Irish people exceedingly. "Oh, Queen dear," one old lady is reported to have shouted, "make one of thim darlints Prince Patrick, and all Ireland will die for ye!" There was another royal baby born in May of the following year, and named Arthur Patrick Albert; but whether or not the Queen took the hint from the old Irishwoman, I really cannot say.

The royal party sailed in the "Fairy" from Cork to Dublin. Here the reception of the Sovereign was really magnificent. There were, of course, triumphal arches, and all sorts of flags and decorations, but the great feature of the scene was the people. "It was a wonderful and exciting scene," says the Queen in her diary, "such masses of human beings, so enthusiastic, so excited, yet such perfect order maintained; then the number of troops, the different bands stationed at certain distances, the waving of hats and handkerchiefs, the bursts of welcome which rent the air—all made it a never-to-be-forgotten scene, when one reflected how lately the country had been in open revolt and under martial law." As the royal carriage passed under the last triumphal arch, "a poor little dove," says the Queen, "was let down into my lap, with an olive branch around its neck, alive, and very tame."

There were grand reviews and drawing-rooms and so forth in Dublin, and then the Queen went to the Duke of Leinster's place; here, in the park, she was much amused at seeing the country people dancing Irish jigs.

On leaving Dublin, when the steam-yacht passed the end of Kingstown pier, which was densely packed with spectators, the Queen mounted the paddle-box and stood beside Prince Albert, waving her hand; then, at her command the engines were stopped, and the Royal Standard was three times lowered as a parting salute. Then the yacht sailed through stormy weather to Belfast, where there was another joyful reception, after which the party crossed over to Scotland. The passage across was exceedingly rough. The Queen says, "Poor little Affie was knocked down and sent rolling over the deck, and was completely drenched." "Affie," of course, was Prince Alfred, now Duke of Edinburgh.

After her return to London, the Queen was to have gone to open the New Coal Exchange, but she was prevented by an attack of chicken-pox. So Prince Albert went with the Prince of Wales and the Princess Royal in the old Royal Barge, "a gorgeous structure of antique design." The Lord Mayor followed in the City Barge, and other gaily decorated vessels helped to make up a gay river procession.

Fortunately for all concerned in this novel water pageant, the day, although late in October, was fine and bright. The Royal party enjoyed a remarkable spectacle as they were rowed down the stream by twenty-seven watermen in rich liveries, under the command of Lord Adolphus Fitzclarence. All the barges and steamers and lighters on the river were loaded with human beings to their utmost capacity, and the banks were everywhere densely crowded. The very streets running down from the Strand were so thickly packed with spectators, that each one, seen from the water, presented the appearance of a moving mass. It was calculated that to witness the unwonted sight at least half a million of persons were gathered together. Over all the bridges they seemed to be clustered like swarms of flies, and ever and anon the air was rent by the long and far resounding shouts of welcome.

The Royal visitors landed at the Custom House Quay, and walked under coloured canvas through crowds of citizens to the Coal Exchange. The Recorder, in his big cloak and wig, read an address in loud tones, and it is said that the Prince of Wales looked " struck and almost awed by his manner," especially when the tall official looked down at that little boy, not quite eight, and called him " Your Royal Highness, the pledge and promise of a long race of kings." Lady Lyttelton says, " Poor Princey did not seem to guess at all what he meant." But the two children evidently enjoyed their first experience of public ceremonials, and after the banquet, as they were returning to the State Barge, Prince Albert said to them, " Remember, you are indebted to the Lord Mayor for one of the happiest days of your lives."

On December 2nd, Queen-Dowager Adelaide died, after many years of suffering. Our young readers will remember that this was the Queen's Aunt Clarence, referred to towards the beginning of this little book. Queen Victoria saw her for the last time a few days before the close. Her Majesty says: "There was death written in that dear face. It was such a picture of misery and of complete prostration, and yet she talked of everything. I could hardly command my feelings when I came in, and when I kissed twice that poor dear thin hand. . . . I love her so dearly; she has ever been so maternal in her affection to me. She will find peace and a reward for her many sufferings." In accordance with her own wish, Queen Adelaide was "without pomp or state," laid by the side of King William's coffin at Windsor, and ten sailors of the Royal Navy attended to its last resting-place the coffin containing the remains of her who had been the bride of the Sailor-King.

DUBLIN CUSTOM HOUSE.

TO COMMEMORATE
THE VISIT
OF HER MOST GRACIOUS MAJESTY
QUEEN VICTORIA
TO THIS PARK
OCTOBER 10ᵗʰ 1851
AND HER RECEPTION
BY MORE THAN
EIGHTY THOUSAND
SUNDAY SCHOOL TEACHERS & SCHOLARS

INAUGURATED
BY HIS ROYAL HIGHNESS
THE PRINCE ALBERT
MAY 9ᵗʰ 1853

STATUE OF HER MAJESTY IN PEEL PARK.

THE EXHIBITION OF 1851.

CHAPTER XIV.
" ALL NATIONS " IN HYDE PARK.

PRINCE ARTHUR.

DURING 1850, Prince Albert was working hard to bring about his grand idea of an Exhibition of the Industry of All the World. We shall see presently how this idea was realised in the following year.

Meanwhile, on May-day, 1850, Prince Arthur William Patrick Albert was born. Prince Albert wrote of the event to a relation at Coburg, telling how

1

the little boy had been "received by his sisters with *Jubilates.* 'Now we are as many as the days of the week,' was the cry, and a bit of a struggle arose as to who was to be Sunday. Out of well-bred courtesy, the honour was conceded to the new comer. Victoria is well and so is the child."

In the Autumn, the Queen visited Scotland, and for the first time slept in her ancient Palace of Holyrood. The Queen saw the work-table and other relics of her famous ancestress, Mary of Scotland, and of course, that staircase from the chapel, up which came Ruthven and his fellow conspirators to the murder of David Rizzio in Mary's presence. A day was spent in drives about Edinburgh, and then to dear Balmoral, " to strengthen our hearts," as Prince Albert says, "amid the stillness and solemnity of the mountains."

The great event of the year 1851, in England, was of course the Exhibition. We have got used to International Exhibitions now, and we dare say our young readers will find it difficult to understand why we were all so excited in 1851. Some of us whose beards are getting grey now, were in our teens then, and can well remember how we were thrilled with enthusiasm when all the peoples of the earth came to Hyde Park, at the invitation of Prince Albert, to join in the peaceful rivalry of science and art. All that we fondly dreamed of, as regards peace and progress, did not come to pass; but undoubtedly commerce, invention, industry, and zeal for knowledge received a quickening impulse, the vast importance of which it would be impossible to estimate.

In May, 1851, all the world seemed to be represented in London. Costumes of every land were visible; the language of every land was heard in the streets. The gathering of all nations was the great idea that seemed to be occupying everyone's mind. It is said, that a street-boy seeing and hearing two foreigners engaged in violent altercation, shouted out, " Go it, all nations ! " and then stood to watch the anticipated fight.

Like a fairy palace, there sprang up in Hyde Park the transparent walls and roof of the great building in whose grand transept the lofty trees of the park stood untouched. It would trespass too much on our space to begin telling of the triumphs of art and skill that adorned the First International Exhibition. Before the opening, the Queen paid a private visit. On her return she wrote: " We remained two hours and a half, and I came back quite beaten, and my head quite bewildered from the myriads of beautiful and wonderful things which now quite dazzle one's eyes. Such efforts have been made, and our people have shown such taste in their manufactures. All owing to this Great Exhibition, and to Albert— all to *him !* "

On May-day, the Exhibition was opened with a State ceremony. The Queen's own narrative of the events of the day is so touchingly interesting, that there needs no apology for our quoting it. She writes : "May 1st. The great event has taken place, a complete and beautiful triumph, a glorious and touching sight, one which I shall ever be proud of, for my beloved Albert and my country . . . . Yes, it is a day which makes my heart swell with pride and glory and thankfulness.

"We began it with tenderest greetings for the birthday of our dear little Arthur. At breakfast, there was nothing but congratulations. . . . Mamma and Victor (the Queen's nephew) were there, and all the children and our guests. Our humble gifts of toys were added to by a beautiful little bronze *replica*, of the Amazon, from the Prince (of Prussia), a beautiful paper knife from the Princess (of Prussia), and a nice little frock from Mamma.

"The Park presented a wonderful spectacle, crowds streaming through it, carriages and troops passing quite like the Coronation Day, and for me the same anxiety; no, much greater anxiety on account of my beloved Albert. The day was bright and all bustle and excitement. . . . The Green Park and Hyde Park were one densely crowded mass of human beings in the highest good humour and most enthusiastic. I never saw Hyde Park look as it did, as far as the eye could reach. A little rain fell just as we started, but before we came near the Crystal Palace, the sun shone and gleamed upon the gigantic edifice, upon which the flags of all the nations were floating.

HER MAJESTY DECLARING THE EXHIBITION OPEN.

We drove up Rotten Row, and got out at the entrance on that side.

"The glimpse of the transept through the iron gates, the waving palms, flowers, statues, myriads of people filling the galleries and seats around, with the flourish of trumpets as we entered, gave us a sensation which I can never forget, and I felt much moved. We went for a moment to a little side room, where we left our shawls, and where we found Mamma and Mary (now Duchess of Teck), and outside which were standing the other Princes. In a few seconds we proceeded, Albert leading me, having Vicky at his hand, and Bertie holding mine. The sight as we came to the middle, where the steps and chair (which I did not sit on) were placed, with the beautiful crystal fountain in front of it, was magical—so vast, so glorious, so touching. One felt, as so many did whom I have since spoken to, filled with devotion, more so than by any service I have ever heard. The tremendous cheers, the joy expressed in every face, the immensity of the building, the mixture of palms, flowers, trees, statues, fountains, the organ (with six hundred instruments and two hundred voices, which sounded like nothing), and my beloved husband, the author of this peace festival, which united the industry of all nations of the earth—all this was moving indeed, and it was and is a day to live for ever. God bless my dearest Albert! God bless my dearest country, which has shown itself so great to-day! One felt so grateful to the Great

God, who seemed to pervade all and to bless all.
The only event it in the slightest degree reminded
me of was the Coronation, but this day's festival
was a thousand times superior.

" Albert left my side after 'God Save the Queen'
had been sung, and at the head of the Commissioners, a curious assemblage of political and

THE CHINESE AMBASSADOR AT THE OPENING OF THE EXHIBITION, 1851.

distinguished men, read me the Report, which is a
long one, and to which I read a short answer;
after which the Archbishop of Canterbury offered
up a short and appropriate prayer, followed by
the Hallelujah Chorus, during which the Chinese
Mandarin, He-Sing, came forward and made his
obeisance.   This concluded, the procession began.

It was beautifully arranged, and of great length. . . . The whole long walk from one end to the other was made in the midst of continued and deafening cheers, and waving of handkerchiefs. Everyone's face was bright and smiling, many with tears in their eyes. Many Frenchmen called out 'Vive la Reine!' . . . The old Duke (of Wellington) and Lord Anglesey walked arm in arm. I saw many acquaintances among those present. We returned to our own place, and Albert told Lord Breadalbane to declare that the Exhibition was opened . . . . which was followed by a flourish of trumpets. and immense cheering.

"The return was equally satisfactory, the crowd most enthusiastic, the order perfect. We reached the Palace at twenty minutes past one, and went out on the balcony and were loudly cheered. . . . That *we* felt happy, thankful, I need not say ; proud of all that had passed, of my darling husband's success, of the behaviour of my good people. . . . Albert's name is immortalised, and the wicked reports of dangers of every kind, which a set of people, viz., the *soi-disant* fashionables, the most violent Protectionists, spread, are silenced.

" I must not forget to mention an interesting episode of the day, viz., the visit of the good old Duke (of Wellington) on this, his eighty-second birthday, to his little godson, our dear little boy. He came to us both at five, and gave him a golden

THE QUEEN AND THE SUNDAY SCHOOL CHILDREN IN PEEL PARK.

cup and some toys, which he had himself chosen, and Arthur gave him a nosegay."

The Exhibition season was a very brilliant one for the Londoners.   One of its gayest events was the " Restoration Ball," at Buckingham Palace.   All those invited had to come in the dress of the time of Charles II.   Along with diamonds and Honiton lace, the profuse display of ribbons of all colours was the great feature of the occasion ; festoons of ribbons adorned the wristbands, and hung down from the waistcoats of gentlemen.   Mr. Gladstone was rather quietly dressed in " a velvet coat turned-up with blue satin, ruffles and collar of old point, black breeches and stockings, and shoes with spreading bows."   He represented Sir Leoline Jenkins, a judge in King Charles' time.   There was a grand ball to which the Queen came, at the Guildhall, in July, when the City gave her a splendid reception.

Towards the end of August the Royal Family went to Balmoral.   The Queen did not travel so fast then as now; she stopped a night at the Angel Inn, Doncaster, and another night at her palace of Holyrood.   On her return, in October, the train was delayed near Forfar, through the over-heating of the axle of a carriage truck, and, subsequently, between Glasgow and Edinburgh, a pipe connected with the engine burst.   The royal train was enveloped in steam, and had to wait an hour in a curved cutting.   The Edinburgh officials, who were waiting for the train, became terribly uneasy, and sent off a pilot engine to the rescue. The *Annual Register* records that during the misadventure " Her Majesty exhibited the greatest composure and patience."

The Queen returned to London by way of Liverpool. Thick mists and heavy rain did their best to spoil everything as the Queen drove through the principal streets and inspected the Docks, but immense crowds loyally defied the weather, and fifty thousand flags floated above the shipping. Her Majesty then proceeded to Manchester, where she was delighted with the long rows of millworkers, " dressed in their best, ranged along the streets with white rosettes in their button-holes." But in Peel Park, the crowning incident of the day took place. Eighty-two thousand Sunday school children of all denominations were collected there, and after an address had been received by the Queen in her carriage, they raised their youthful voices in unison and sang " God Save the Queen." Altogether the Queen saw that day at least a million of her subjects.

Before the close of the Exhibition, the Queen paid a few more visits to it. Six million two hundred thousand visitors entered its doors. The Queen mentions in her diary, Mary Kerlynack, who had walked all the way up from Cornwall, nearly three hundred miles, to see the Exhibition and the Queen. She stood at one of the doors and saw the Queen pass out. "A most hale old woman," says Her Majesty, "who was near crying at my looking at her."

On October 15th, Prince Albert closed the Exhibition. "How sad and strange to think this great and bright time has passed away like a dream."

Not a single accident had occurred during the whole time the Exhibition had been open, although six million two hundred thousand persons had visited it. The receipts amounted to half a million of money.

This year 1851, saw before its close, the death of the King of Hanover, the last surviving son of George III. In December, there came fearful news from Paris, Louis Napoleon, the President of the French Republic, deliberately broke his most solemn promises, and by the murder or banishment of thousands of French men and women, bore down all opposition to his ambitious schemes and got himself made Perpetual President. He subsequently changed his title to that of Emperor.

THE SWISS COTTAGE, OSBORNE.

CHAPTER XV.

In the Isle of Wight.

THE Queen had a beautiful seaside residence built at Osborne, in the Isle of Wight. Here the Royal Family enjoyed a more quiet and retired life than was possible at Buckingham Palace or Windsor. Osborne is indeed a charming home, such as any monarch might well be proud of. From the seabeach the terraced ground rises till on the highest terrace, amidst bright flower gardens and fountains

and statuary, stands the stately mansion with its
two lofty towers. On the lower terrace, where the
myrtles and magnolias, camellia bushes, and ilexes
flourish, are groves and shrubberies. The corridors
and rooms within the building, with their luxurious
furniture and adornments, the painting, statuary
and richly stocked cabinets, and the magnificent
views of sea and land we must not linger over.
Extensive grounds surround this princely home on
the land side, and here (as well as on the terraces),
Prince Albert found an ample field for the
exercise of his wonderful talent for landscape
gardening.   On   every   hand   are   seen   the
impress of his taste and skill.   He always looked
forward with joy to going to Osborne.   "We shall
go," he says in one letter, "on the 27th, to the Isle
of Wight for a week, where the fine air will be of
service to Victoria and the children; and I, partly
forester, partly builder, partly farmer, and partly
gardener, expect to be a good deal upon my legs
and in the open air."   On another occasion the
Queen writes from Osborne : "Albert is so happy
here—out all day planting, directing, etc.; and it
is so good for him.   It is a relief to be away from
all the bitterness people create for themselves in
London."

On the first evening after the Royal Family
moved into their new home by the sea, there was
a grand house-warming festival.   Prince Albert
repeated the hymn sung in Germany on such
occasions, and which was written by Martin

Luther. The first verse of the English translation, is :—

"God bless our going out, nor less
Our coming in, and make them sure ;
God bless our daily bread, and bless
Whate'er we do—whate'er endure ;
In death unto His peace awake us,
And heirs of His salvation make us."

The Queen commemorated one of her birthdays at Osborne, by putting the children in possession of the Swiss Cottage and its grounds, situated about a mile from the Palace, on the extensive Osborne estate. The Swiss Cottage stands "brown and picturesque, with its deep overhanging eaves, and German inscription carved below the sloping roof, duly held on by big stones. In front of it lie, all in a row, the nine gardens of the nine children of the Queen." The place was not intended simply as a playhouse and playground. Besides their flower gardens there were also vegetable gardens, greenhouses, hothouses, forcing frames, etc., for the children to attend to for two or three hours a day, under the direction of a gardener. Each of them had a set of tools, duly marked with the name of the owner. For all work done the children received from the gardener a certificate, which they presented to Prince Albert, and received the exact market price for their labour. Of course, these earnings were something additional to their regular allowances of pocket money. There was a carpenter's shop for the boys, who also, under their

K

father's directions, constructed a very perfect small fortress. For this fortress the princes did all the work with their own hands, even to the making of the bricks.

For the young princesses, the lower portion of the Swiss Cottage was fitted up as a kitchen, with pantry, closets, dairy and larder, all as complete as possible, and here these juvenile Royal Highnesses, dressed *à la cuisinière* and with arms white with flour, learned to make cakes and tarts, and all sorts of plain dishes, to cook the vegetables which they had themselves cultivated, to preserve fruit, and to prepare different sorts of pickles. In fact, they were trained to be good English housewives. Sometimes they partook of the food they had themselves prepared, and sometimes, on very special occasions, invited the Queen and Prince Albert to come and partake of a repast at the Swiss Cottage. But as a rule, the results of the kitchen labours were distributed to the poor of the neighbourhood. From their later positions of exalted State in grand Palaces, no doubt the happiness and fun of those young days have often been fondly looked back to by those who then worked or played side by side in the Swiss Cottage and its pleasant grounds.

But the building we have been referring to also contained a Museum of Natural History, and other curiosities. The greater portion of the contents of this museum had been collected by different members of the Royal Family in their rambles and excursions. There were specimens illustrating botany and geology, stuffed birds and other animals, as well as numerous articles designed and constructed by the children themselves, and various curiosities of which they had become possessed.

Among the various objects in this museum are the clothing of two infants. One set of things was evidently worn by a child whose parents were in good circumstances; the other set com-prises articles of a humbler description. Visitors who obtain permission to inspect the contents of the Swiss Cottage are always attracted by this collection, which awakens a very painful interest. The garments belonged to two infants who were the sole survivors of a shipwreck. The clothes afforded no clue to the parentage of the children, whose origin is thus involved in mystery. Queen Victoria hearing of the circumstance kindly took upon herself the responsibility for the care of the infants. They were reared and brought up on the Osborne estate under Her Majesty's super-vision, and, after being suitably educated, were placed in the Royal Navy.

The poor round Osborne, like the poor round Balmoral, have received much kindness from the Queen and her family. The Queen has, in a quiet way, given personal attention in many cases. A clergyman not many years ago, calling on an aged parishioner near Osborne, found as he entered the invalid's room, that a lady in deep mourning was sitting by the bedside. As he came in, he heard her finish reading a verse from the Bible. He was about to go away, when the lady said: "Pray stay. I should not wish the invalid to lose the comfort which a clergyman might afford." The lady then retired, and the clergyman found lying on the bed a book with portions of scripture suitable for sick persons. From that book the lady in black, who was the Queen of England, had been reading. Many similar circumstances are known to those who have visited amongst the poor in that district.

H.R.H. PRINCE LEOPOLD, DUKE OF ALBANY.

From Photo by Messrs. Downey & Co.]   *[To face Chap. XVI.*

WATCHING THE TROOPS DEPART FOR THE CRIMEA.

CHAPTER XVI.

THE WAR CLOUD.

THE streets of London were thronged with thousands of spectators, clad for the most part in garments of mourning, as with marching squadrons, and with trophies of war and heraldic pomp, the mortal remains of the famous Duke of Wellington were borne, in November, 1852, to the Cathedral of St. Paul's. The news of her great captain's death had come to the Queen in her Highland home. She was in London

at the time of the funeral, and from the balcony
of Buckingham Palace saw the procession pàss
up Constitution Hill, and then again, with her
children grouped about her, saw it from the
windows of St. James's Palace.

In March of the following year, the Queen was
enabled by personal experience to sympathise with
those of her subjects who have ever had their
houses on fire. The Queen was sitting with Prince
Albert in the "White Drawing Room," when an
alarm was raised on account of the smell of smoke
and burning. It was soon found that the upper
stories of the "Prince of Wales' Tower" were what
the firemen call "well alight." Prince Albert and
the gentlemen in the Castle aided in the work of
clearing out the splendid Gothic Dining Room
and the Crimson Drawing Room, which were
threatened with destruction, and all the treasures
were taken out of the jewelled armoury. The
firemen with their engines did their very best, but
it seemed for a time as if Windsor Castle would be
burnt out. At length, after five hours' struggle
with the flames, the danger was past. The Queen
says of it in one of her letters: "Though I was
not alarmed, it was a serious affair, and an
acquaintance with what a fire is, and with its
necessary accompaniments, does not pass from
one's mind without leaving a deep impression.
For some time it was very obstinate, and no one
could tell whether it would spread or not. Thank
God, no lives were lost."

Three weeks after the fire, Prince Leopold George Duncan Albert was born at Windsor. Baby was about two months old when his brother, the Prince of Wales, was laid up with the measles. Prince Albert took it, and was very ill, and then the Princess Royal, and Princess Alice and the Queen all took it successively in a mild form. Some of the guests who came to baby's christening took back the measles with them to the Courts of Hanover, Belgium and Coburg, and for some time people were amused with the way in which this infantile complaint was showing its want of respect for royal families.

Early in 1853 the Queen was much troubled by the false accusations that were made against her husband. The fact was that many people were jealous of Prince Albert's blameless life. He made the Court so pure and respectable that they were angry at not being able to indulge more freely in the vices that they loved. And so they took the opportunity of some disagreement between Lord Palmerston and his colleagues to get up lying rumours about Prince Albert's interfering unlawfully in Government matters, and acting treacherously towards England. Crowds of people actually went to Tower Hill expecting to see the Prince taken to prison. Queen Victoria was very grieved and indignant, but the Prince was very calm, and as soon as Parliament met, Lord Aberdeen and Lord John Russell completely refuted the false charges, and all the politicians and newspapers who had joined in the outcry tried to get their folly forgotten as soon as possible.

The fourteenth anniversary of the wedding-day came, and the Queen wrote : " Fourteen happy and blessed years have passed, and I confidently trust many more will, and find us in old age, as we are now, happy and devotedly united. Trials we must have ; but what are they if we are together ? " There were grand doings at the Palace that fourteenth wedding-day. Baroness Bunsen, who was one of the company, tells us how " that evening between five and six o'clock we followed the Queen and Prince Albert a long way, through one large room after another, till we came to one where a red curtain was let down ; and we all sat in the dark till the curtain was drawn aside, and the Princess Alice, who had been dressed to represent Spring, recited some verses taken from Thomson's *Seasons*, enumerating the flowers which Spring scatters round. And she did it very well ; spoke in a distinct and pleasing manner, with excellent modulation, and a tone of voice like that of the Queen. Then the curtain was drawn and the whole scene changed, and the Princess Royal represented Summer, with Prince Arthur lying upon some sheaves as if tired with the heat and harvest work. The Princess Royal also recited verses. Then again there was a change; and Prince Alfred, with a crown of vine leaves and a panther's skin, represented Autumn, and recited also verses and looked very well. Then there was a change to a winter landscape; and the Prince of Wales represented Winter, with a white beard and a cloak with icicles or snow flakes (or what looked like such), and the Princess Louise, warmly clothed, who seemed watching the fire ; and the Prince also recited well a passage altered from Thomson. Then another change was made, and all the seasons were grouped together; and far behind on high appeared the Princess Helena, with a long veil hanging on each side down to her feet, and a long cross in her hand, pronouncing a blessing on the Queen and Prince in the name of all the seasons. . . . . The Queen ordered the curtain to be again drawn back, and we saw the whole Royal Family; and they were helped to jump down from their raised platform, and then all came into the light and we saw them well. And the baby, Prince Leopold, was brought in by the nurse and looked at us with big eyes, and wanted to go to his papa, Prince Albert. At the dinner table, the Princesses Helena and Louise and Prince Arthur were allowed to come in and to stand by their mamma, the Queen, as it was a festival day."

The War with Russia broke out in February, 1854. I shall say as little as possible about the War in these pages. The English people at the time were delirious with war fever, but all sensible people got ashamed of the whole thing afterwards. The fact was, we joined the French tyrant to fight against the Russian tyrant, for the sake of the Turkish tyrant, who was the worst of the lot.

British soldiers fought bravely, as they always do, but thousands were killed in battle, or died of cold and starvation ; but it would be hard to say "what good came of it at last," except to wicked contractors, who sold rotten provisions and worthless stores to the army, and to newspaper people, who made vast profits by selling news and pictures referring to the war which they had clamoured for.

The Queen saw her soldiers depart, and wished she had one son to send in the army and one in the navy. There was a gay season in London, and happy visits to Osborne, and then came that gloomy winter of 1854-5, when churches and theatres and all places of public resort looked sombre with the mourning garments that so many were wearing. The British Army was besieging the great stronghold of Sebastopol and suffering fearful hardships. The Queen wrote to Lord Raglan about the needless privations to which the soldiers were subjected, and Florence Nightingale and her trained nurses went out and changed the hospitals from dens of horror and despair into abodes of comfort and peace. The Queen's health suffered from her anxieties. When in February, 1855, the Commander-in-Chief, Lord Raglan, paid a flying visit to Windsor, the Royal children told him, "You must hurry back to Sebastopol and take it, or else it will kill mamma."

In April, Queen Victoria's Imperial ally, Napoleon III., came with his beautiful Empress Eugenie to Windsor. · The old queen Amélie, the

widow of the ex-king Louis Philippe, was now
living in England, and visited the Queen and Prince
Albert at Windsor two or three days before the
Imperial party "It made us both so sad," writes
Queen Victoria, "to see her drive away in a plain
coach with miserable post horses, and to think that
this was the Queen of the French, and that six
years ago her husband was surrounded by the same
pomp and grandeur which three days hence would
surround his successor."

On the Emperor's arrival he kissed the Queen's
hand, and she kissed him on both cheeks. They
all seemed very happy together, although the
streets of Paris had so lately ran with blood that
this man might reign, and crowds of his wretched
victims were even now slowly dying in the swamps
of Cayenne. At the grand ball, which followed a
grand review, the Queen felt it strange that she,
"the grand daughter of George III., should dance
with the Emperor Napoleon, nephew of England's
great enemy, now my nearest and most intimate
ally, in the Waterloo Room, and this ally only
sixteen years ago, living in this country in exile,
poor and unthought of."

The Londoners seemed positively wild with enthusiasm when the Emperor and Empress went to
a banquet at the Guildhall, and in the evening
through a "sea of human beings cheering and
pressing near the carriage," in brightly illuminated
streets, to the Opera. On another day, the
Queen took her guests to the Crystal Palace—

where thousands upon thousands of excited spectators seemed to vie with each other in noisy greetings of the illustrious visitors.

Through the summer of 1855, the War was still raging, and the Queen visited two or three  times the invalids and wounded who came home, and dispensed the medals that had been won by bravery. In August, the Queen, accompanied by Prince Albert and the Prince of Wales, returned the visit of the French Emperor; they were shown all the sights of Paris, and greeted everywhere with joyful acclamations. St. Cloud was given up to the English Royal Party as

NAPOLEON III.

a residence during their stay. Visits to the Exhibition, etc., balls, banquets, opera, and what not filled up the time. A grand State Ball at Versailles was a very splendid affair indeed. Queen Victoria made her toilette in Marie Antoinette's boudoir. No ball had been given in this historic Palace since that ball in the Orangery on the night that the Bastille was taken and sacked by

the insurgent people. Altogether, this visit to
Paris (like the Imperial visit to Windsor), seems
to have pleased everybody concerned and to
have gratified both nations. For more than four
hundred years—that is to say, since the infant
King Henry VI. was crowned in Paris—no English
monarch had visited the capital of France. The
two nations had looked upon each other for
centuries as "natural enemies." It was now hoped
that these mutual courtesies (although a Bonaparte
was mixed up in them) might inaugurate " a long
period of mutual goodwill, the interchange of
mutual kind offices, of the products of nature
and art, of the efforts of peace and civilisation."
And so a great many people who felt indignant
when the "Man of December," stained with so
many crimes, kissed the cheeks of our beloved
Queen, they kept silence for the sake of the
peaceful alliance between two great nations. The
enthusiasm of the French as the English Queen
went about amongst them was indescribable. On
the return the Emperor accompanied his illustrious
guests as far as Boulogne, and there the English
Queen witnessed a grand review of the French
army. She must have thought of the vast preparations made by the First Napoleon so near the
same spot for the projected invasion of England,
only sixteen years before her own birth. She had
previously been conducted by the Emperor to the
marble tomb beneath the gilded dome of the In-
valides; and what must have been Queen Victoria's

thoughts as she stood with the nephew in friendly alliance, beside the grave of the uncle, with whom her own family had fought so long as the foe of the human race. The Queen did not fail to explain in the course of a quiet drive, how impossible it would be for her to break off with her friends of the Orleans family in their reverses. The Emperor expressed himself to be fully satisfied.

Sebastopol was taken in September, and the news was brought to the Queen, then at Balmoral. Then Prince Albert and all the gentlemen and servants went to the top of the hill, and the keepers and ghillies and villagers came flocking from far and near. They lit an enormous bonfire, which the Queen watched from her Palace window, and all about the bonfire there was dancing and shouting, and piping and gun-firing, and squib-lighting and whisky drinking, for joy that the English flag was at length floating above those hitherto impregnable ramparts.

MISS NIGHTINGALE AND THE CRIMEAN WOUNDED.

CHAPTER XVII.

DOMESTIC EVENTS.

HOLYROOD.

TO Queen Victoria's palace home among the Scottish hills, in the summer of 1855, came Prince Frederick William of Prussia, to woo the Princess Royal of England. The young man was twenty-four, "the little lady" (as Prince Albert calls her) only fifteen. On the heathery side of Craig-na-ban the Prussian Prince one day plucked a piece of white heather (the emblem of good luck) and gave it to the Princess. And then words were spoken on the subject that both had been thinking about, and the young couple agreed to tread life's pathway side by side. The wedding was not to be for two years yet, but the young Prince came as often as he could to see his promised bride.

March, 1856, brought the signing of the treaty of peace with Russia, and great were the rejoicings, attended with gun-firing and bell-ringing and grand illuminations. In April, 1857, the last of Queen Victoria's babies was born at Buckingham Palace. Prince Albert, writing to Coburg, says the baby "is thriving famously, and is prettier than babies usually are. . . . She is to receive the historical, romantic, euphonious and melodious names of Beatrice Mary Victoria Feodora."

It was decided that the Princess Royal should be married on January 25th, 1858, and Buckingham Palace was filled with gay and illustrious wedding guests as the day approached. The expectant bridegroom had visited England several times in the interval. He was in this country when an accident occurred that might have robbed him for ever of his promised bride. The Princess Royal was sealing a letter when her muslin sleeve caught alight. Her governess, Miss Hildyard, was sitting near her, and Princess Alice was with her music-mistress in the same room. They at once got the hearthrug round the Princess Royal, and extinguished her blazing dress. The arm was burnt from below the elbow to the shoulder, but no serious result followed. Lady Blomfield tells us, "When the Princess burnt her arm she never uttered a cry; she said, 'Don't frighten mamma, send for papa first.'"

The wedding day came, and about thirty princes and princesses, and three hundred peers and peeresses, assembled in the old chapel of St. James's Palace. We read that the bride looked " very touching and lovely, with such an innocent, confiding, and serious expression, her veil hanging back over her shoulders." There were eight bridesmaids " in white tulle, with wreaths and bouquets of roses and white heather." A few days afterwards the happy husband took his English bride away to his Prussian home. Thousands of people lined the streets, and many of us can well remember the tear-swollen face of the Princess as she drove in an open carriage through the falling snow. The grief at parting with her mother and sisters, for the time overpowered every other emotion. Her father, with " Bertie " and Alfred, accompanied her to Gravesend.

But even the weeping Princess was obliged to laugh when someone in the crowd shouted, " If he doesn't treat you well, come back to us! " There was no doubt, however, about her being well treated, and she became very popular at the Prussian Court. On the evening after her public entry into Berlin she had to polonaise with twenty-two princes in succession. The Princess Frederick William (as she was now called) was a good deal annoyed at first with the stiff etiquette of the Prussian Court. But she learned to put up with what could not be helped, and resolutely broke through those rules which she felt were too absurd to be put up with.

I am not writing the life of the Princess Royal,

but I must stay to tell one or two anecdotes about her, because they illustrate the character of the Royal Lady who is the proper subject of this book. A Prussian Princess, it appeared, might not carry chairs about, but on one occasion the Countess Perponcher, a very venerable and important personage, discovered our Princess in the act of carrying a chair across a room and setting it down in another corner. The Countess earnestly remonstrated. "I'll tell you what, my dear Countess," said the English Princess, "you are probably aware of the fact of my mother being Queen of England?" The Countess bowed in assent. "Well," said the Princess, "then I must reveal to you another fact. Her Majesty, the Queen of Great Britain and Ireland, has, not once, but very often, so far forgotten herself as to take up a chair. I speak from personal observation, I can assure you. Nay, if I am not greatly deceived, I noticed, one day, my mother carrying a chair in each hand, in order to set them for her children. Do you really think that my dignity forbids anything which is frequently done by the Queen of England?"

The Countess Perponcher was dismayed on another occasion at finding the Princess arranging and putting away a quantity of linen. "My mother did it," was again an answer to all objections.

But we must hasten back to England, where, from this time, Princess Alice took her sister's place in the Royal circle. Baby Beatrice, as the

latest comer, now attracts much attention. Prince
Albert writes: "Little Beatrice is an extremely
attractive, pretty, intelligent child; indeed, the
most amusing baby we have had." Another time
he says: "Beatrice on her first birthday looks
charming, with a new light blue cap. Her table of
birthday gifts has given her the greatest pleasure,
especially a lamb."

In May, 1858, Prince Albert went to see his
married daughter, and in the Autumn he went
again, accompanied by the Queen. Concerning
the meeting the Queen says: "There on the
platform stood our darling child, with a nosegay
in her hand. . . . She stepped in, and long and
warm was the embrace as she clasped me in her
arms; so much to say, and to tell, and to ask, yet so
unaltered; looking well, and quite the old Vicky
still."

The Queen was again on the Continent in
September, 1860, and met at Coburg her daughter,
the Princess Royal, who was now the happy
mother of a little Prince and Princess. During
this journey an accident occurred to Prince Albert.
He was by himself in an open carriage, when the
four horses that were drawing it suddenly took
fright and galloped wildly at full speed towards
the adjacent railway line, where, in front of a bar
guarding a level crossing, stood a waggon. The
Prince saw that a crash was inevitable, and leaped
out, happily escaping with a number of cuts and
bruises. The driver stuck to his seat, and when

the collision occurred, was thrown out and seriously hurt. One horse was killed on the spot, the others galloped along the road to Coburg. Colonel Ponsonby, the Prince's equerry, happened to meet them, and seeing that something had happened, at once procured a carriage and got two doctors to accompany him to the scene of the accident. They found the Prince doing the best he could for the injured man, and Colonel Ponsonby was sent to give the Queen the first account of the affair. In her deep gratitude for the preservation of the Prince, Her Majesty founded a charity for helping young men and women in their apprenticeships, setting up in business, and marriage.

Before the year was over, Prince Louis of Hesse Darmstadt was at Windsor to win Princess Alice for his bride. The betrothal was soon arranged to the entire satisfaction of all parties; but two years, marked by sad changes, were to pass away before the wedding could be celebrated.

H.R.H. PRINCESS OF WALES ON BOARD THE ROYAL YACHT, OSBORNE.[1]

From Photograph by Symonds & Co.]

[To face Chap. XVIII.

CHAPTER XVIII.

SORROW UPON SORROW.

IN the unpretending mansion of Frogmore, near to the grey towers of Windsor, dwelt the venerable mother of Queen Victoria, in failing health, and cared for and watched over with the utmost tenderness. The Duchess of Kent was now

seventy-five years of age ; her health had for some time grown more and more delicate, but there was no special cause for immediate anxiety till March, 1861. Alarming symptoms appeared; the Queen and Prince Albert hastened to the bedside of the aged sufferer; there was a long sad night of anxious watching and then all was over—"her gentle spirit at rest, her sufferings over."

The Queen was very much affected by her mother's death. Prince Albert writes: "She is greatly upset and feels her childhood rush back upon her memory with the most vivid force. Her grief is extreme. . . . For the last two years her constant care and occupation have been to keep watch over her mother's comfort, and the influence of this upon her own character has been most salutary. In body she is well, though terribly nervous . . . she remains almost entirely alone."

In the retirement of Osborne, the Queen gradually overcame the first excess of grief, and became more resigned; but a cloud of sadness seemed from this time to shadow her life. Her birthday that year was kept without the usual festivities. In the summer there was a visit to Ireland and the beautiful lakes of Killarney, and subsequently a sojourn at Balmoral, and some delightful Highland excursions. Towards the end of the year what is known as the "Trent" affair occurred. It was whilst the southern portion of the United States was in rebellion, trying to form an independent nation, of which, as they said, slavery should be the chief corner stone! Two of the rebels were coming to Europe on board the English steamer "Trent," to try and make mischief between

England and the United States. An American captain stopped the "Trent" on its way to England, and took the rebel envoys prisoners. Of course, he had no right to do this, and the English Government and people were very indignant. Lord Palmerston, in his usual bullying way, wrote a fierce and threatening remonstrance—one that would probably have plunged the two nations concerned into war. But the Queen and Prince Albert toned it down into something more conciliatory, yet quite as dignified. The result was that the United States Government at once repudiated the rash action of the naval captain, and set the two prisoners free.

His amicable efforts, in conjunction with Her Majesty, to bring about a peaceful settlement of this "Trent" affair, were the last public service in the beneficent life of "Albert the Good." He had been for some time far from well; and on December the 2nd the doctors saw symptoms of low fever.

For a few days there were alternations of hope and fear, whilst the Prince strove resolutely against his illness, and refused to go to bed and be regularly laid up. The Queen and Princess Alice read to him. But the symptoms grew more decidedly dangerous, and the anxious Queen went through her State duties as one "in a dreadful dream." On December 8th, the Prince was removed at his own request to a larger and brighter room—it happened to be the one in which both William IV. and George IV. had died. That day

was Sunday, and Charles Kingsley preached at the
Castle, but the Queen sadly notes in her diary that
she "scarcely heard a word."

Of this day, one of the Queen's household, in a
letter written shortly afterwards, says: "The last
Sunday Prince Albert passed on earth was a very
blessed one for Princess Alice to look back upon.
He was very weak and very ill, and she spent the
afternoon alone with him while the others were at
church. He begged to have his sofa drawn to the
window that he might see the sky and the clouds
sailing past. He then asked her to play to him,
and she went through several of his favourite
hymns and chorales. After she had played some
time, she looked round and saw him lying back,
his hands folded as if in prayer, and his eyes shut.
He lay so long without moving that she thought
he had fallen asleep. Presently he looked up and
smiled. She said, 'Were you asleep, dear Papa?'
'Oh, no,' he answered, 'only I have such sweet
thoughts.'

"During his illness his hands were often folded
in prayer; and when he did not speak, his serene
face showed that the 'sweet thoughts' were with
him to the end."

The fortitude and devotedness of Princess Alice
all through this trying time was something that
neither the Royal Family nor the nation ever
forgot. She shed no tears in her father's presence,
but sat by him, conversed with him, and repeated or sang hymns, and when she could bear

it no longer, calmly walked to the door and rushed off to her room, returning presently with her calm sad face showing no traces of the agitation she had gone through.

It was on the afternoon of Saturday, the 14th of December, that it became evident that the end was approaching. *" Gutes Frauchen "* were his last loving words to the Queen as he kissed her, and then laid his head against her shoulder. Some time afterwards the Queen bent down and said : *" Es ist kleines Frauchen ;"* the Prince knew her and bowed his head in answer. Quietly and without suffering he continued to sink, and at a few minutes before eleven o'clock he ceased to breathe. Soon after midnight, the solemn tones of the great bell of St. Paul's sounded over the City, proclaiming that a Royal Prince had gone to his eternal rest.

The favourite hymn of the Prince in his last illness had been the well known one, beginning—

> "Rock of Ages, cleft for me,
> Let me hide myself in Thee."

To a physician who expressed the hope that he would be better in a few days, he said : " No, I shall not recover; but I am not taken by surprise ; *I am not afraid ; I trust I am prepared."* For six months before his death (as the Queen afterwards stated), his mind had often dwelt on death and the future state ; they had often conversed together upon such topics, and he had been much interested in a book called *Heaven our Home*, which they had read together.   He had once remarked, "We don't know in what state we shall meet again; but that we shall recognise each other, and be together in eternity, I am perfectly certain."

When referring to her bereavement, the Queen said she was a wonder to herself, and she felt sure that she had been so sustained in answer to the prayers of her people.   "There's not the bitterness in this trial that I felt when I lost my mother—I was so rebellious then; but now I can see the mercy and love that are mingled in my trial."

But for a time it seemed as if the Queen would speedily follow her husband.   For some days she was prostrate with weakness, and her pulse could hardly be felt.   Hope revived, when it was at length announced that Her Majesty had had some hours' sleep.   They took her as soon as possible to the quiet home at Osborne, and with solemn rites they laid the body of the Prince in the Royal Chapel at Windsor, whence it was afterwards transferred to a splendid mausoleum built by the Queen in the grounds of Frogmore.

Princess Alice was the right-hand of the Queen in the first sad months of bereavement, and the chief means of communication between the Sovereign and her Ministers.   But Her Majesty soon roused herself to her high duties, whilst evermore shrinking from State ceremonials and the mere splendours of royalty as much as possible. Her own sorrows did not make her pass by

unnoticed the sorrows of others, and before the
first month of her widowhood had passed she was

THE ROUND TOWER, WINDSOR.

telegraphing from Osborne her "tenderest sympathy for the poor widows and mothers" left

desolate, when upwards of two hundred miners perished in the terrible Hartley Colliery accident.

Of the way in which the Queen has discharged her Royal duties during her long widowhood, Lord Beaconsfield has plainly spoken : " There is not a dispatch received from abroad, or sent from this country abroad, which is not submitted to the Queen. The whole of the internal administration of this country greatly depends upon the sign-manual of our Sovereign, and it may be said that her signature has never been placed to any public document of which she did not know the purpose and of which she did not approve. Those Cabinet Councils of which you all hear, and which are necessarily the scene of anxious and important deliberation, are reported on their termination, by the Minister to the Sovereign, and they often call from her critical remarks requiring considerable attention ; and I will say, that no person likely to administer the affairs of this country would be likely to treat the suggestions of Her Majesty with indifference, for at this moment there is probably no person living who has such complete control over the political condition of England as the Sovereign herself."

HER MAJESTY AT THE WEDDING OF THE PRINCE OF WALES AT WINDSOR.

[To face Chap. XIX.

PRINCESS ALEXANDRA AND HER ELDEST CHILDREN.

CHAPTER XIX.

THE COMING OF ALEXANDRA.

PRINCESS ALICE.

THE marriage of Princess Alice to the Prince of Hesse at Osborne, on a July afternoon in 1862, was a very quiet affair. The bridesmaids were the sisters of the bride and bridegroom; the Queen, in deep mourning, was present at the service only. In three hours the wedding was completed and the guests had all departed.

There was a visit to Balmoral and another to Coburg this summer, both reviving many mournful memories. The Queen was much touched by a present that arrived before the close of the year. It was a richly-bound Bible, presented through the Duchess of Sutherland—an offering from "many widows of England." In acknowledging this gift, the Queen expressed her heartfelt thanks to her "kind sister-widows," and after speaking of her consolations in sorrow, added, "That our Heavenly Father may impart to 'many widows' those sources of consolation and support, is their broken-hearted Queen's earnest prayer."

The month of March in the following year (1863) will be long remembered by all who witnessed the coming of the fair Alexandra, the "Sea-King's daughter from over the sea," to be the bride of the Prince of Wales.

I must not stay to tell how the London streets and bridges were glorious with flags, garlands, arches, banners, streamers, floral devices, national emblems, medallions, and other decorations too numerous to mention. Thousands upon thousands of spectators filled the air with acclamations as the gay procession came on, escorting the open carriage in which sat the Prince of Wales and his beautiful bride. One of the most thrilling spectacles along the route occurred when the thousands of ladies ranged on tiers of scarlet-covered seats beside St. Paul's Cathedral stood up amongst that forest of flags and wreaths and orange-blossoms, whilst deafening cheers resounded from St. Paul's School and all the adjacent footways and windows and

THE PRINCE OF WALES AND PRINCESS

FROM A CONTEMPORARY PORTRAIT, 1863.

house-tops. The Princess gave one glance upward at the mighty dome, and then, visibly affected by the enthusiasm of the myriad of spectators, bowed repeatedly with much feeling, winning all hearts by her graceful and modest beauty.

Meanwhile, at a window of Windsor Castle, Queen Victoria and her two youngest daughters waited till dusk for the coming of the expected ones. They came at last, reaching the grand entrance at half-past six, and in a few minutes the Princess Alexandra was in the loving arms of the Queen, who met her on the grand staircase. All who were about the Queen soon declared that the Queen's affections had never before been so suddenly and so warmly called out by any one. The charming Danish Princess fell at once into her place as one of the Queen's children, and became the favourite of the Royal Family and of the English nation.

The wedding took place at St. George's Chapel, Windsor, three days after the arrival. There was a grand display of rank and beauty, and the solemn rites were duly performed amidst all the stately pageantry of a royal marriage. But the widowed Queen sat apart in the royal pew, from which she could look down on the ceremony; she was attired in the simplest and plainest of widow's caps, a black silk dress, with white collar and cuffs, and black gloves. The star and blue riband of the Order of the Garter formed the only relief to her sombre garb.

I need not linger over the wedding ceremonies. That night London and many other towns were brilliantly illuminated; everywhere there was festivity and rejoicing, and everybody felt with the poet :—

> " Sea-King's daughter, as happy as fair,
> Blissful bride of a blissful heir,
> Bride of the heir of the Kings of the Sea,
> O, joy to the people and joy to the throne,
> Come to us, love us, and make us your own !
> For Saxon, or Dane, or Norman we,
> Teuton, or Celt, or whatever we be,
> We are each all Dane in our welcome of thee,
> Alexandra ! "

After a short visit to Germany, the Queen was at her Highland home in September. On a previous visit Her Majesty and the elder Princes and Princesses had each placed a stone on the summit of Craig Lowrigan, as part of the foundation for a cairn in memory of Prince Albert. That cairn had now been completed—a pyramid of granite, thirty feet high, plainly to be seen for many miles round. It bore the inscription, " To the beloved memory of Albert the Great and Good, Prince Consort, raised by his broken-hearted widow, Victoria R."

An alarming accident befel the Queen in October. She was returning with two of her daughters from Altnagiuthasac one dark evening, when suddenly in the midst of the wild moorland the carriage was upset. The Queen was thrown out with her face on the ground, but escaped with some bruises and a hurt to one of her thumbs. The rest of the party

M

escaped uninjured. After the traces had been cut, the ladies sat down, sheltered by the overturned carriage, and waited whilst the coachman went off for assistance. Half-an-hour passed, and then the anxious listeners heard the sound of approaching hoofs and of voices. They soon found it was their own ponies, which had been sent away before the accident. But the servant who was in charge of them had become anxious on account of the Queen not appearing, and had ridden back to see what was the matter. So the Queen and Princesses were glad to mount the ponies, which were led home to Balmoral, where Her Majesty found her two sons-in-law waiting at the door, wondering at the delay, but as yet knowing nothing of its cause.

In the following week the Queen made her first public appearance since her husband's death. It was to unveil a statue of him at Aberdeen. His splendid mausoleum at Frogmore was now approaching completion. Her Majesty spent altogether more than two hundred thousand pounds from her own private purse on this splendid tomb and on the Albert Memorial Chapel at Windsor. The latter edifice, originally built for Cardinal Wolsey, has been adapted by the Queen to its present purpose. A pedestal of beautiful Pyrennean marble supports a magnificent white marble cenotaph, with kneeling angels and allegorical figures. The recumbent statue of Prince Albert represents him as a knight in armour, with the favourite hound, Eos, at his feet.

The armour is symbolical, for the epitaph is, "I have fought the good fight, etc." All around, the Chapel is lavishly adorned with rich mosaics, stained glass, fretted marble, medallions and other decorations. The Frogmore Mausoleum contains the famous statue of the Prince by Baron Marochetti.

In the summer of 1865, we find the Queen and her children present at the unveiling of a statue of Prince Albert at Coburg. More than one royal personage in Europe wanted to be present; but the Queen replied that the occasion was one of strictly domestic interest, and the presence of strangers would be unacceptable. In the square of the little town stood the gilt bronze statue, ten feet in height, the right hand resting on a plan of the Great Exhibition. Luther's hymn, "*Ein feste Burg,*" was sung, and then the Queen, approaching the statue, handed her bouquet to be laid on the pedestal; the Princesses and other ladies followed her example, till the fragrant offerings rose high about the feet of the statue.

During the autumn visit to the Highlands in this year, Her Majesty visited the Duchess of Athole. The journey was at first through heavy mists, and then through pouring rain. In the twilight the coachman lost his way, and the whole party were in the midst of a thick wood. The two attendants had to go before with a coach lamp to find a way out. At nine o'clock they reached the cottage of the Duchess, at Dunkeld, and at dinner the Queen tried the famous Scotch dish, "haggis," and says she liked it very much.

Early in 1866 the Queen opened Parliament for the first time since Prince Albert's death. But as she entered there was silence instead of the customary flourish of trumpets, and the robes of State, instead of being worn, were laid upon the throne. The Prince of Wales sat on her right hand, and on her left stood the Princesses Helena and Louise. The Speech was read by the Lord Chancellor. During the same year, Her Majesty instituted the "Albert Medal," for the saving of life at sea; reviewed the troops at Aldershot; created Prince Alfred Duke of Edinburgh; and attended the weddings of Princess Mary of Cambridge to the Duke of Teck, at Kew, and of Princess Helena to Prince Christian, at Windsor.

War broke out in Germany, and the Queen had the pain of seeing her married daughters on different sides. Princess Alice at her home in Darmstadt heard the Prussian cannon, and dreaded every hour to hear the news of her husband being among the slain. At length the quiet little town was taken; pestilence broke out in the hospitals crowded with wounded, but Princess Alice worked as long as her strength held out, with other Hessian ladies, to help and comfort the sufferers. At length, in the very room in which its father's banner lay hidden, the third daughter of Princess Alice was born. But peace was proclaimed, and in token that the plague of war was stayed, the babe was named Irene.

The Queen again opened Parliament in person in 1867, and laid the foundation stone of the Albert Hall. Her Majesty published her book, *Leaves,* *etc.,* (to which I have referred in connection with the circumstances described in it), early in 1868. She sent a copy to Charles Dickens, and wrote in it that it was a gift "from one of the humblest of writers to one of the greatest." In May she laid the foundation stone of St. Thomas's Hospital, and reviewed 27,000 volunteers in Windsor Park; and in July visited Switzerland. On her return she proceeded to Balmoral: and here let me mention that the *Leaves from our Life in the Highlands* refer to the visits to Scotland during Prince Albert's lifetime. Her Majesty has recently published a book entitled *More Leaves, etc.,* giving an account of her Highland experiences during her widowhood. It contains very many interesting passages, one or two of which may be now referred to.

The Queen had a cottage built for occasional residence at Glassalt Shiel. She thus tells of the house-warming in October, 1867: "At twenty minutes to ten we went into the little dining room, which had been cleared, and where all the servants were assembled. We made nineteen altogether. Five animated reels were danced, in which all but myself joined. . . . Then Grant made a little speech, with an allusion to the wild place

we were in, and concluding with a wish 'that our
Royal Mistress, our good Queen,' should 'live
long.' This was followed by cheers given out by
Ross, in regular Highland style, and then all
drank my health. This merry, pretty little ball
ended at a quarter past eleven; the rest, however,
went on singing in the steward's room for some
time, and all were very happy, but I heard
nothing, as the little passage near my bedroom
shuts everything off."

On another occasion Her Majesty describes
watching the process of "juicing the sheep," that
is, dipping them in a trough full of a mixture of
soap and tobacco juice, "a curious and picturesque
sight." Visits to the poor, the christening of
foresters' children, death-bed scenes in lowly
cottages, sheep-shearing, and numerous other
scenes and incidents are simply and graphically
spoken of in *More Leaves*, and there are many
descriptions of romantic Highland scenery. At
Fergusson's Inn, the Queen says, "Here lives Mrs.
Fergusson, an immensely fat woman, and a well-
known character, who is quite rich and well
dressed, but will not leave the place where she has
lived all her life selling whisky. She was brought
out, and seemed pleased to see me, shaking hands
with me and patting me."

The Queen's solitude was generally respected,
but there were some exceptions. During an
excursion to the scene of the Glencoe massacre,
she says, "We sat down on the grass, we

three "—(the Queen, Princess Beatrice and Lady
Jane Churchill)—" on our plaids, and had our
luncheon, served by Brown and Frankie, and then
I sketched. The day was most beautiful and calm.
Here, however—here in this complete solitude—we
were spied upon by impudently inquisitive reporters,
who followed us everywhere; but one in particular
(who writes for some of the Scotch papers) lay
down and watched with a telescope, and dodged
me and Beatrice and Jane Churchill, and was most
impertinent when Brown went to tell him to move,
which Jane herself had thought of doing. However, he did go away at last, and Brown came back
saying he thought there would have been a fight,
for when Brown said quite civilly that the Queen
wished him to move away, he said he had quite as
good a right to remain there as the Queen. To
this Brown answered very strongly, upon which
the impertinent individual asked, ' Did he know
who he was ?' and Brown answered he did, and
that ' the highest gentleman in England would not
dare to do what he did, much less a reporter,' and
he must move on, or he would give him something
more. And the man said, ' Would he dare say
that before those other men (all reporters) who
were coming up?' and Brown said, ' Yes, before
anybody who did not behave as he ought.' More
strong words were used, but the others came up
and advised the man to come away quietly,
which he finally did." Of course, this man must
have been a specimen of the lowest class of

reporters; no respectable journalist would have behaved so.

The Queen has always been partial to dogs. She writes one day, " My favourite collie, Noble, is always downstairs when we take our meals, and was so good, Brown making him lie on a chair or couch, and he never attempted to come down without permission, and even held a piece of cake in his mouth without eating it till told he might. He is the most 'biddable' dog I ever saw, and so affectionate and kind; if he thinks you are not pleased with him, he puts out his paws and begs in such an affectionate way."

The Queen had a sincere friend and highly valued counsellor in Dr. Norman McLeod. In many passages of her journal she speaks very warmly of his friendship, and of the way in which he taught her resignation, and " cheered and comforted and encouraged" her in the early years of her great sorrow. Dr. McLeod writes of one of his frequent visits to Balmoral: " After dinner, the Queen invited me to her room, where I found the Princess Helena and the Marchioness of Ely. The Queen sat down to spin on a fine Scotch wheel, while I read Burns to her—' *Tam O'Shanter* and *A Man's a Man for a' that*'—her favourites." When this good man died and the Queen remembered all his friendship and sympathy and Christian teaching, she deeply felt how " this too, like so many other comforts and helps, was for ever gone."

AT HOME, OSBORNE.

From a photo by]   *[Messrs. Hughes & Mullins, Ryde.*

PORTION OF EAST PANEL, ALBERT MEMORIAL.

CHAPTER XX.

ILLNESS OF THE PRINCE OF WALES, ETC.

MARQUIS OF LORNE.

VERY briefly must I now touch upon the principal events of Queen Victoria's reign during the period that has not yet been touched upon. In November, 1869, the loyal people of London rejoiced to see their Queen engaged in a public ceremony after so long an absence. She came on this occasion to open Blackfriar's Bridge and the Holborn Viaduct. It was a cold but bright day, and the Queen, accompanied by Prince Leopold and her younger daughters, drove through the crowded streets in an open carriage. The Queen was still in mourning robes, and the band of crape was on one arm of each of her servants.

The Queen came to London again in May, 1870, and opened the new buildings of the University of London. During this year the terrible Franco-German War was raging—the Queen's sons-in-law were fighting against her intimate friends, Napoleon and Eugenie. At one period of the war her daughter, Princess Alice, was visiting the four hospitals in Darmstadt daily. There were no less than twelve hundred wounded Frenchmen being nursed in that little town.

Next year the Queen opened Parliament; whilst the Chancellor read her speech, she sat "quite still, her eyes cast down, only a slight movement of the face." In March, Princess Louise was married at Windsor to the Marquis of Lorne. The Queen herself gave away the bride, who "was very pale, but handsome, as she always is" (so writes Lord Ronald Gower, who was "best man" at the wedding). Rice and white satin slippers were showered after the happy pair when they drove away to spend the honeymoon at Claremont, and John Brown threw a new broom after them, Highland fashion.

The frontispiece to this volume represents her Majesty as she appeared at this period. It is a reproduction of the beautiful photograph taken by Mr. Downey.

Towards the close of the following year, the Queen and her people were united in a common anxiety on account of the alarming illness of the Prince of Wales. It was on her return in November, from Balmoral, that the Queen was informed that her son was lying ill with typhoid fever at Sandringham. The Queen went and stayed with him for a few days, but returned to Windsor early in December as all seemed to be going on favourably. The patient was devotedly nursed by his wife, the Princess of Wales, Princess Alice (who happened fortunately to be on a visit at Sandringham when the fever showed itself), and the Duke of Edinburgh. There was a relapse on December the 8th, and the Queen and all the Royal Family were sent for to Sandringham.. The Prince seemed for many days hovering between life and death. Deep and universal was the intense sympathy of the nation, and those who saw it will never forget the reading of the bulletins posted up at the Mansion House. In all the churches and chapels, prayers were offered for the Prince on the bed of sickness and for his distressed wife and mother. On the night of Wednesday, the 14th, a date which some had dreaded as the anniversary of Prince Albert's death ten years previously, there was a slight improvement, the patient was able to sleep, and from this time the gradual recovery went forward.

The period of convalescence lasted, however, into

AT TEMPLE BAR, THANKSGIVING DAY, 1872.

February, and the 27th was fixed upon as a day of Thanksgiving for the Prince's complete recovery. It was at first intended to be a private service for the Queen and her household, but it became a national festival. The Queen and Prince came from Buckingham Palace to St. Paul's along streets thronged with people—footways, shops, windows, doorsteps, porticos, balconies, and in many cases the very roofs were occupied by enthusiastic spectators. Lofty stands and galleries rose in tiers wherever practicable, and overhead banners and streamers and strings of flowers hung from side to side of the decorated streets. All along the route countless pennants floated from Venetian masts, and mottoes and floral devices, and wreaths and trophies were everywhere.

The multitude cheered heartily and the school children sang hymns as the pale Prince passed by and continuously bowed his acknowledgments. The Queen had white flowers in her bonnet, and looked happier than her people had seen her for ten years past. In the great Cathedral, specially adorned for the occasion, and arranged to seat 13,000 persons representing all that was eminent or distinguished in the State—the solemn service of thanksgiving took place. In the evening London was brilliantly illuminated, and the very dome of St. Paul's was marked out by three girdles of coloured lights.

On the following day, as already mentioned, the Queen was shot at by a half-crazy Irish lad. This

intensified the loyal feeling that had already been
so universally excited. In a letter to her people
on February the 29th, the Queen says : "Words
are too weak for the Queen to say how very deeply
touched and gratified she has been by the immense
enthusiasm and affection exhibited towards her
dear son and herself, from the highest down to the
lowest, on the long progress through the capital.
. . . The remembrance of this day will for ever
be affectionately treasured by the Queen and her
family."

In May of the following year the Queen received
very trying news from Hesse. Her little grand-
son, Prince Frederick, died through an accident.
Princess Alice was in bed and the nurse had
brought the two little children to see their mother,
and had left them playing beside her. The
windows both in the bedroom and in the adjoining
dressing room were wide open. The elder of the
two, Prince Ernest, wandered into the dressing
room, and Princess Alice at once rose and hurried
after him. Her absence was but momentary, but
in that time, little Prince Frederick, then rather
more than two years of age, leaned out of one of
the windows of the bedroom, over-balanced himself, and fell on to the stone pavement beneath. He
was terribly injured and in a few hours he died.

In January, 1874, the Queen had to welcome
another daughter-in-law, for her second son, the
Duke of Edinburgh, was married at St. Peters-
burg to the Grand Duchess Marie of Russia. On

March 12th, the young couple entered London; the Queen and the Duchess, with the bridegroom and his sister, Princess Beatrice, drove slowly through the crowded streets in a carriage and six, in spite of a heavy snowstorm. Perhaps to the Russian Princess the snow only made it look more homelike.

In August, 1875, as the Royal yacht was crossing from the Isle of Wight to Gosport, the yacht "Mistletoe" ran across its bows. A collision took place, and the unfortunate "Mistletoe" turned over and sank. The sister-in-law of the gentleman who owned the yacht was drowned. The crew were rescued, but the master, an old man, died soon afterwards from the effect of a blow received from a falling spar. The Queen was sitting on deck at the time of the accident; she was of course greatly distressed at the occurrence, and personally aided in the efforts that were made to restore one of the sufferers.

Lady Augusta Stanley (who formerly, as Lady Augusta Bruce, had been in personal attendance on the Queen from 1846 to 1863), died, after a lingering illness, in March, 1876. The Queen had long been warmly attached to her, and like all who knew her admired her noble and beautiful life. Dean Stanley (the now widowed husband), was also numbered amongst the Queen's personal friends. Her Majesty attended the funeral and afterwards led the widowed mourner into his now desolate home in the Abbey precincts. She after-

N

THE ALBERT MEMORIAL, KENSINGTON.

wards caused a memorial cross in memory of Lady Augusta Stanley to be placed in the grounds of Frogmore.

The magnificent Albert Memorial, beside Kensington Gardens, was completed in the Spring of 1876. This year also the Queen unveiled a statue of the Prince Consort, at Edinburgh, on which occasion the old city was very gay and lively. In the evening there was a grand banquet at Holyrood Palace, where the Queen met a great gathering of the Scotch nobility—Bruces, Murrays, and Primroses, Scots and Kerrs, etc. Soon afterwards, at Ballater, she gave new colours to the " Royal Scots," a regiment of which when she was born her father was the colonel.

On New Year's Day, 1877, Queen Victoria was proclaimed Empress of India with great pomp and ceremony at Delhi and other Indian cities. In February, she received a very remarkable present from the Empress of Brazil. This was a dress woven entirely of spiders' webs, and for fineness and beauty no silk dress could be at all compared with it.

Just before the close of this year, the Queen and Princess Beatrice visited Lord Beaconsfield, at Hughenden, and had lunch there; before they left, the Royal visitors each planted a tree on the lawn. On this occasion the little town of High Wycombe seized the opportunity to almost smother itself in flags and festoons and triumphal arches. There was hardly room for another flag or motto anywhere. The people shouted and the children sang, and the bells rang incessantly, and the whole of the two miles' drive from Wycombe station to Hughenden Manor was a scene of intensest enthusiasm. The good folks hereabouts are very clever at making chairs of beechwood, which grows luxuriantly in the neighbourhood. So one of the triumphal arches was made entirely of chairs of all sorts very artistically piled up. It was so curious that the Royal carriage was stopped for the Queen and Princess to have a good look at it.

Passing over State affairs, and military and naval reviews and so forth, we find the Queen's life during 1878, again shadowed by a great sorrow, and one in which the nation fully sympathised with her. On the 14th of December, the anniversary of her father's death, Princess Alice breathed her last at the early age of thirty-five. Diphtheria had broken out among the Royal Family of Hesse Darmstadt, and had attacked all its members one after another. The Princess Marie, aged four, died in November. Four weeks afterwards, the mother who had devotedly tended her husband and children passed away. The funeral was attended by two of her brothers, the Prince of Wales and Prince Leopold, but nobody was pleased at hearing that for fear of infection, her elder sister, the Crown Princess of Germany, was forbidden to join the circle of mourners. The torchlight funeral was a very imposing solemnity; the townsfolk of Darmstadt stood in mournful silence as their beloved Grand Duchess was carried to the tomb. In England very wide-spread signs of mourning gave evidence of the place in the national heart which had been won by the Princess, whose life had been so marked by self-sacrifice and anxious care for the well-being of others.

I might fill many pages with stories of the Princess Alice, and I must just find room for one. The Princess liked to get rid of all fuss and ceremony whenever it was possible to do so. An English lady of high position residing at Darmstadt, one day received a note from the Princess saying that she would call and take tea with her the following afternoon. Scarlet cloth, as etiquette seemed to demand, was laid down, and a man was sent to the top of the house to watch for the Royal carriage and give due notice of its approach, so that the Princess might be received at the entrance with all due honours. But up to the time named by the Princess, no carriage of any kind had come in sight. Suddenly a ring at the street door was heard, and a lady attired in a waterproof and wearing goloshes made her appearance. " I have made a point," she said, " of not treading on your beautiful scarlet cloth ; " and she intimated that in future she should be glad to be received, not as a Royal Princess making a State visit, but as a private lady "dropping in " upon a friend.

During this year, 1878, the Queen's cousin, the blind King of Hanover, died in exile at Paris. Another family event was the marriage of her

grand-daughter, Princess Charlotte of Prussia,
(daughter of the Princess Royal). In May next
year, the Princess Charlotte was the mother of a
little Princess, so Queen Victoria was now a great
grandmamma. A little before this occurred, Princess Marguerite of Prussia had come to England
to be married, on March 13th, to the Duke of
Connaught, the Queen's third son. There was
a very grand wedding indeed at Windsor, the
grandest that had taken place since the marriage
of the Princess Royal, and the Queen took her full
part in the proceedings. The bride was given
away by her father, in his Hussar uniform of
brilliant scarlet; this was "the Red Prince," who
had been so conspicuous at Konigrätz and Sedan.

The Queen was much distressed when at Balmoral this summer, by hearing that the young
Prince Imperial had been killed in the Zulu War.
His father, driven from the throne of France, had
found in England an asylum and a grave. The
sorrow-stricken mother soon came northward to
meet her sympathising friend, Victoria of England,
whose own near relations had been among the
Emperor's deadliest foes. The fugitive Empress,
weeping over her great and irreparable loss in
the retirement of Abergeldie, confessed, " I have
been too favourable to war."

From the diary of the Queen's sojourn in the
Highlands this autumn of 1879, we learn how a
cairn was built to commemorate the Duke of
Connaught's wedding. The Queen writes under

date of September 8th : "A fine morning. Breakfasted with Beatrice, Arthur and Louischen, in
the garden cottage, and at eleven we started for
Arthur's Cairn, I on my pony, 'Jessie,' Beatrice
walking to the top. We were met by Arthur and
Louischen, and went on to near the Cairn. I got
off when we were near it ; and here were assembled
all the ladies and gentlemen, also Dr. Profeit, the
keepers and servants belonging to the place, with
their families, and almost all our servants from the
house." Then follow particulars of the drinking
of "healths," which appears to have been the
general accompaniment of these ceremonies. The
Queen continues : "Fern (who, with the other dogs,
was there) resented the cheering, and barked very
much. We all placed a stone on the cairn, on
which was inscribed, 'Arthur, Duke of Connaught
and Strathearne, Married to Princess Louise
Margaret of Prussia, March 13th, 1879.' After
a few minutes we left, I walking down the whole
way. We stopped at Dr. Profeit's on my way
down, and here I got on my pony again."

I must pass on over 1880 and 1881, except just
to say that when President Garfield was shot at,
the Queen united in the anxious solicitude that
was felt all over the world for the noble soul that
was struggling so long between life and death.
When all was over, she telegraphed at once to
Mrs. Garfield, "Words cannot express the deep
sympathy I feel with you in this terrible moment.
May God support and comfort you as He alone

can." She also wrote, not through a secretary, but in her own handwriting, a sympathising letter to Mrs. Garfield, as she had done twenty years before to the widow of Abraham Lincoln, when that great man was assassinated.

Prince Leopold was married to Helen of Waldeck at Windsor, in April, 1882. In the following month the Queen and Princess Beatrice went in State to Epping Forest, and it was formally dedicated to the people's use for ever. The Lord Mayor and Corporation of London, who had spent a great deal of money to get large tracts of forest land away from the persons who were trying to steal it from the public, were all there in State.

Of course Prince Leopold had to take his bride to Balmoral that autumn. The young couple were met at Ballater Station, and escorted home. "The pipes preceded" (says the Queen) "playing the 'Highland Laddie,' Brown and all our other kilted men walking alongside, and before and behind the carriage, everybody else close following; and a goodly number they were. We got out at the door and went just beyond the arch, all our people standing in a line, headed by our Highlanders. . . . . Dr. Profeit gave Leopold and Helen's healths, and after these had been drunk, Brown stepped forward and said nearly as follows: ' Ladies and Gentlemen,—Let us join in a good Highland cheer for the Duke and Duchess of Albany; may they live long and die happy!'

which pleased every one, and there were hearty cheers."

To Prince Leopold, a little daughter was born in 1883, but in April, 1884, that child was fatherless. The refined and scholarly Duke of Albany was never strong, and was at Cannes on account of his health when he died. The Queen, who had herself experienced bereavement in its most trying forms, kept down her natural grief as a mother, to go and minister to the young widow at Claremont.

In 1885 the youngest of the Queen's daughters, Beatrice Mary Victoria Feodora, was married to Prince Henry of Battenberg, in Whippingham Church, near Osborne.

The General Election of 1885 being completed, the Queen came to London in the early days of 1886 to open the first Parliament in which all classes of Her Majesty's subjects were actually represented.

The Queen's life has been of late a very retired one, and her people were glad to see her once more the centre of a public pageant. An immense concourse of people hailed her with acclamations as the bright procession, with its splendid escort of the Royal Horse Guards, swept on its way from Buckingham Palace through St. James's Park, and then past historic Whitehall and the venerable Abbey to the Peers' entrance of the House of Lords. As usual, eight cream-coloured horses drew the State Chariot of the Queen. The

House of Lords, with its painted windows and frescoes and golden ornaments, presented an imposing aspect when Peers in scarlet and ermine, and Peeresses aglow with jewels, filled its area. Then, attended by high officers of State, Queen Victoria passed to her throne ; a few of the Commons scrambled into the small space which is (for the present) assigned to them, and the Lord Chancellor read Her Majesty's speech.

My story of the Queen's life is nearly finished. She still reigns over us, and long may it be ere anyone may be able to complete the history of her reign. A few miscellaneous anecdotes and sketches are reserved for the closing chapter.

ALBERT MEMORIAL, EDINBURGH.

IN ST. PAUL'S CATHEDRAL, THANKSGIVING DAY, 1872.　　[To face Chap. XXI.

CHAPTER XXI.

WITH a few anecdotes about the Queen, or those immediately connected with her, we shall bring our little book to a close.

One day, as the story goes, two of the Princesses, when very young, happened to go into a room in which a servant was engaged in polishing a grate. In a spirit of frolicsome mischief the girls insisted on helping her, and then when they had got possession of the brushes, instead of polishing the grate, they polished the woman's face. The servant knew that she could not get away from that

range of apartments without encountering Prince
Albert, and was overwhelmed with confusion.
The Prince, on seeing the poor woman with her
black face coming from his apartments, enquired
the reason, and the servant reluctantly told him.
The Queen was of course soon made aware of the
circumstance, and she was presently seen crossing
the court towards the servants' quarters, leading
the two Princesses by the hand. The woman (who
by this time had probably washed her face) was
brought forward, and Her Majesty then made her
daughters ask the servant's pardon for their offence.
In the next place, they were both sent at once to
the nearest drapery and millinery establishment,
and compelled to purchase for the woman, out of
their own pocket-money, a complete outfit—dress,
bonnet, shawl, gloves, etc.—as a reparation for the
dress that had been soiled by the blacklead spilt
over it. The two Princesses afterwards declared
that they didn't care in the least for having had to
spend their money in making presents to the
woman, in fact they rather enjoyed it than other-
wise, but it was having to ask the woman's pardon
that they didn't like. With all forms of distress
and suffering the Queen has shown a benevolent
sympathy, and she has exerted her influence,
when possible, on behalf of the oppressed. When
a draft treaty, arranging for peace and commerce
between England and Madagascar was sent out,
the Queen wrote on the margin, "Queen Victoria
asks as a personal favour to herself, that the Queen

of Madagascar will allow no persecution of the Christians." In the treaty sent back, signed a short time afterwards, the words occur, "In accordance with the wish of Queen Victoria, the Queen of Madagascar engages that there shall be no persecution of the Christians in Madagascar."

On occasions of great disaster or widespread calamity, such as fires, colliery explosions, railway collisions, etc., the Queen has sent kindly messages to the surviving sufferers and the bereaved ones, and when substantial aid was required, has set a good example by contributing to the relief of those needing it. One of her first public acts after her own sad bereavement, was a visit in May, 1863, to Netley Hospital, of which she and Prince Albert had laid the foundation stone seven years before. On this foundation stone Her Majesty on entering gazed first for a few seconds, and then proceeded through the wards. To those who seemed most ill she went and spoke, and showed a very kind interest in their condition. An old Irish soldier from India lay nearly at the point of death. After the Queen had spoken to him, he said: "I thank God that He has allowed me to live long enough to see Your Majesty with my own eyes." Both the Queen and Princess Alice, who accompanied her, were very much touched by this speech, which came so evidently from the very heart of the dying man. The Queen passed through long lines of invalid soldiers from India and other parts, bowing to them kindly as she passed along. The

Queen's appearance at this time is thus described by an eye witness: "When she is silent, her face is sad and bears the marks of a heartfelt and abiding sorrow. Her smile is, however, as gracious as ever, and her voice, though low and very gentle, has all its old sweetness and clearness."

A narrative showing the Queen's kind consideration for those in her employment has been made public. It refers to the orphan daughter of a Scottish clergyman who was engaged as governess to the Royal children. During her first year at Windsor her mother was taken seriously ill, and feeling her first duty was by her mother's bedside, the young lady wished to resign her situation. The Queen would not hear of this, and tenderly told her to go home, stay with her mother as long as it was needful, and then return. In the meantime, said Her Majesty, "the Prince and I will hear the children's lessons; so in any case let your mind be at rest."

The governess for several weeks attended on her dying mother, and then had to lay her beneath the churchyard sod. She returned to the duties in the Palace, and the Queen did not forget with kind womanly sympathy to try and alleviate the young woman's deep sorrow. Every day Her Majesty visited the schoolroom, and the young pupils were exceedingly kind. When the first anniversary of her great loss came round, the governess could scarcely bear her feelings of lonely bereavement in the midst of that great household. She had to begin the day's duties, as usual, by reading a portion of Scripture in the schoolroom. Some words of divine tenderness touched her grieving heart so keenly as she read them that her strength gave way, and laying her head on the desk before her, she burst into tears, saying, "Oh! mother, mother!" The children quietly passed from the room to tell their mother what had happened. It at once flashed on the Queen's mind that it was the anniversary of the poor girl's bereavement. Her Majesty went at once to the schoolroom and said, "My poor child, I am sorry the children disturbed you this morning; I meant to have given orders that you should have had this day entirely to yourself. Take it as a sad and sacred holiday —I will hear the lessons of the children." And then she added, "To show you that I had not forgotten this mournful anniversary, I bring you this gift," clasping on her arm a beautiful mourning bracelet, with a locket for her mother's hair, marked with the date of her mother's death.

The first time that the "Swedish Nightingale," Jenny Lind, sang before the Queen in private, she was accompanied by the Queen's pianist, who is said to have been actuated by some paltry prejudices, and to have taken liberties with the music, which very much annoyed the singer. Her Majesty's quick musical ear instantly detected what was going on. As Jenny stood up to sing the second time, the Queen motioned the pianist aside and said quietly, "I will accompany Miss

FOUR GENERATIONS.
H.M. THE QUEEN.   H.R.H. Princess Henry of Battenberg (Princess Beatrice).
Princess Louis of battenberg (daughter of Princess Alice) and her infant.

Lind." This time the singer had no need to feel that there was the slightest want of harmony between the instrumental and the vocal music.

The Queen's high esteem of the sacred scriptures is evinced by an anecdote that many of our readers may be already familiar with. It was a noble and beautiful answer, says the *British Workman*, that our Queen gave to an African Prince, who sent an embassy with costly presents and asked her to tell him the secret of England's greatness and England's glory; and our beloved Queen told him not of her fleet, of her armies, of her boundless merchandise, or of her inexhaustible wealth. She did not, like Hezekiah in an evil hour, show the ambassador her diamonds and her rich ornaments, but handing him a beautifully-bound copy of the Bible, she said, "Tell the Prince this is the secret of England's greatness."

In the Queen's diary are some passages about preachers. In October, 1854, she writes: "We went to kirk as usual at twelve o'clock. The service was performed by the Rev. Norman McLeod, of Glasgow, and anything finer I never heard. The sermon, entirely extempore, was quite admirable; so simple, and yet so eloquent, and so beautifully argued and put. The text was from the account of the coming of Nicodemus to Christ by night (St. John, chapter iii). Mr. McLeod showed in the sermon how we all try to please *self*, and to live for *that*, and in so doing found no rest. Christ had come not only to die for us,

O

but to show us how to live. The second prayer
was very touching, his allusions to us were so
simple, saying after his mention of us, ' Bless
their children.' It gave me a lump in my throat,
and also when he prayed for ' the dying, the
wounded, the widows, and the orphans.' "

In the following year the Queen heard the Rev.
J. Caird, who, she says, " electrified all present
by a most admirable and beautiful sermon, which
lasted nearly an hour, but kept one's attention
riveted." The text was Rom. xii. 11, "Not slothful
in business ; fervent in spirit ; serving the Lord."
The Queen adds : " He explained in the most
beautiful and simple manner what real religion
is ; how it ought to pervade every action of our
lives ; not a thing only for Sundays or for our
closet ; not to drive us from the world ; not 'a
perpetual moping over good books' ; but 'being
and doing good,' letting everything be done in a
Christian spirit. It was as fine as Mr. McLeod's
sermon last year, and sent us home much edified."

There are many passages in the Queen's journal
showing her anxiety to be faithful in the government and training of her little ones. She kept
them as much as possible under her own care,
till the increasing demands upon her time and
attention of State duties and loyal hospitality
forced her to leave to others much that, as a
loving mother, she would have preferred to do
herself. Speaking of the Princess Royal when a
child, she says : "It is a hard case for me that my

THE QUEEN AT THE LONDON HOSPITAL.

occupations prevent me from being with her when she says her prayers."

Her Majesty, however, exercised extreme care in the choice of those to whom she committed the sacred task of instructing and training her children. The following instructions for the governess of the Princess Royal may be profitably read and thought over by everyone, young or old. "I am quite clear that she should have great reverence for God and for religion; but that she should have the feeling of devotion and love which our Heavenly Father encourages His earthly children to have for Him, and not one of fear and trembling; and that thoughts of death and an after life should not be represented in an alarming and forbidding view; and that she should be made to know as yet no difference of creeds, and not think that she can only pray on her knees, or that those who do not kneel are less fervent or devout in their prayers."

During Her Majesty's visit to the London Hospital in 1876, a little sick girl in the children's ward cried out to the nurse, "Please do let me see the Queen; I shall be quite better if I see the Queen." This request was communicated to the Rev. Mr. Rowsell, Her Majesty's Chaplain, who told the Queen. Immediately Her Majesty did that which pleased her people not a little when the tale was told. She desired to be conducted to the bedside of the child, and there spoke loving words of tenderness and sympathy.

LONDON : KNIGHT, PRINTER, MIDDLE STREET, E.C.